Infected Rage

The Rage Trilogy: Book 3

by

William Blackwell

Cover Designed by Telemachus Press, LLC
Published by Telemachus Press, LLC
ISBN: 978-1-0697318-2-1 (paperback)
Version: 2017.01.01

Acknowledgements

Heartfelt thanks to my loyal readers and supporters, the hardworking staff at Telemachus Press, and Winslow Eliot. Special thanks to The Government of Prince Edward Island for its financial support.

To Lily, for being such a positive influence in my life.

When death, the great reconciler, has come, it is never our
tenderness that we repent of, but our severity.
–T.S. Eliot

Infected Rage

The Rage Trilogy: Book 3

Prologue

Rain pelted the windshield as the killer drove east along Highway 17, occasionally glancing at the Atlantic Ocean. The rough waters and black clouds hovering above suited his mood. He wanted to finish his work and get the hell off this island. He preferred the beaches and the climate of the Caribbean to anything Canada had to offer. But he knew he still had a lot to do before he could escape to his tropical paradise.

In the back seat, the metal cage clattered as the black cat hissed, meowed and jerked spasmodically. The killer glanced back and yellow eyes regarded him threateningly. The cage inched along the back seat of the black Crown Vic, pushed by the feral animal's frantic escape attempts.

"It won't be long now," he tried to reassure the captive animal. It continued hissing and snarling, clawing at the small metal door of its prison.

Finally he arrived at Highway 347 and turned left. The moon glowed full in the grey light of dusk.

He pulled into an empty parking lot by the beach. A cafeteria and a tourist observation deck were the only visible signs of human intervention. The sign in the cafeteria window said *CLOSED*.

He parked, killed the ignition, reached into the glove box and located a thick pair of leather gloves. He put them on and exited the car, glancing around. Save for a few faraway glowing yellow dots—house lights—he was alone.

The cat hissed and snarled as he snatched the cage and carried it out to the beach. He pulled his baseball cap down over his eyes as a sudden chilly wind gust almost blew it away. *Don't be stupid. Can't leave any evidence.*

The black cat had begun to thrash violently against the cage. He set it on the sand, and with a powerful gloved hand, quickly unclasped the metal door. As the cat leaped to its freedom, the killer stepped back and felt the cold steel comfort of his nine millimeter Glock, just in case the crazed animal decided to turn on him. He didn't like to leave anything to chance. He wouldn't hesitate to kill it, even though he knew it would ruin the entire operation.

But the crazed feline leaped out, ran a few feet, stopped abruptly, glanced back and regarded its captor with glowing yellow eyes before hissing and vanishing into the night.

Battered by the wind and rain, the killer returned to his car. He speed-dialed a number on a disposable cell phone and a husky male voice answered.

"It's done," the killer said.

"Any problems?"

"None."

The line went dead.

Chapter One

The color drained from Kathleen Freeborne's face as she gripped the calloused hand outstretched on the table. Then the dark images hit her like a fully loaded semi-truck, invading her calm mind with a violent swirl of emotions that blindsided her. The images: evil horned demons, laughing maniacal madmen, murder, mayhem, tortured souls, screams and blood.

So much blood, so much suffering, and so much death.

She shuddered and tried to release her hand from the bulky, gray-bearded man whose eyes locked hers with a penetrating stare. Jonathon Crawley's eyes were looking right into her soul, and she could tell from his expression they did not like what they saw.

He squeezed tighter as she tried to withdraw her hand. She squirmed in her seat, unable to free her hand from the mammoth meat hook. The macabre images grew more focused and palpable, the screams of the damned louder and more piercing. A cacophony of suffering, gut-wrenching cries for help.

She felt the life force draining from her body, and something else. A rage boiling up inside her, demanding her to smack Jonathon Crawley hard in his sixty-nine-year-old weathered face. She pushed at the rage, trying to force its rising temperature below the boiling point, cool it off somehow—contain its visceral force.

Deep breaths. Calm. You are the lake, calm and still and composed. Snap out of it! Snap out of it, please!

Crawley's face reddened, veins bulging in his neck. A large one snaked across the side of his temple, pulsating as he winced and started grinding his teeth. Kathleen could see the rage also rising up in him. His eyes and expression suggested deadly intentions.

He wants to kill me. Not if I kill him first. No. Force the rage back. You can do this. You have to do it.

Suddenly his grip loosened and she snapped her hand free. She rubbed the painful red splotches that had appeared. It was going to leave a bruise.

Crawley's demeanor slowly softened and the cacophony of misery and anger evaporated from her mind in a flash. "What the hell just happened?" he said.

The color slowly returned to Kathleen's face and her cheeks glowed red from the sudden infusion of blood. She could see he had some haunting memory of what had just happened, but was reluctant to acknowledge its eerie presence. The veins in his neck and head began to shrink.

"There is some scary evil presence at work in you," she said. There was no point in beating around the bush.

After all, she was a clairvoyant, a psychic to whom the residents of Prince Edward Island—and in particular the small town of Montague—paid good money to for her expertise. Crawley would be coughing up $150 for his thirty-minute session, so there was no point in shooting him a line of bullshit.

Or sugar coating things, for that matter.

He wiped his crinkled brow. "What evil presence? I came to you because I've been feeling some dark moods lately, but nothing like what just happened."

"I know. But I felt it. And I can't put a finger on it. I'm not getting any visions that might determine its cause. Not yet anyway, but I'll let you know if I do."

"You mean something might come to you?"

"Yeah, it often does, but sometimes much later." This was only half true, but she didn't know what else to say. Usually, she could see events in the future was able to suggest areas of her clients' lives that they might want to change. Sometimes she could predict positive occurrences and they would leave elated. Other times, she saw terrible things and they left deflated and depressed. In those cases she usually suggested certain avoidance techniques to change the course of their destiny.

Sometimes it worked.

Sometimes it didn't.

Like when thirty-two-year-old Emily Flowers walked into her office and Kathleen took the woman's hand and saw a picture of a semi-truck mowing her down on the highway while she was walking her dog. She had warned Emily not to walk her dog on the highway—not to go near the highway on foot—and that advice had lasted for a week. Then one day Emily's German Shepherd, Butch, jumped the fence surrounding the small rural acreage and ran off down the highway. Without thinking, Emily decided to search for the errant canine. A few minutes later an overworked truck driver barreling down the highway had jerked the steering wheel just slightly as he wiped his sleepy eyes. The vehicle swerved onto the shoulder for only a split second—but long enough to slam Emily like a rag doll across the grill and windshield, killing her instantly. When the truck driver stopped, what remained of Emily's body slithered down the vehicle and landed on the road in a clump of bones, tissue, blood and intestines.

It was then that Butch had appeared from a nearby bush, scampered up to the remains and started whimpering.

"Is there anything you can tell me that might help?" Crawley asked.

Kathleen thought for a moment. His rage, like an infection, had transferred to her, making her want to kill him. Yes, it was more than just slap him. She had wanted to take an axe and slice it right through his head. Put him out of his rage-filled misery. That thought scared her. She wondered if he was contagious, if he could go around infecting the whole town with his condition. She dreaded what might happen if he could. "I think you should stay home until I figure this out."

"I can't do that. I have friends, things I like to do."

Kathleen knew that Jonathon, recently widowed, was still going through a grieving period. His forty-two year marriage had ended abruptly when his wife died of a sudden heart attack nine months earlier. He had a small family support group and many friends in the community. She often saw him at Tim Hortons, sipping coffee with his buddies and trading stories. He now lived alone in his modest home in Montague. She couldn't imagine what it would be like to lose someone who has been in your life intimately for forty-two years.

But she knew only too well what it was like when your boyfriend of four years gets his brains blown out by a shotgun in the hands of a demented old witch. And that was, how many months ago now, maybe six? Never mind his grieving period. She was going through a grieving period of her own.

"Let me ask you this: Do you want to risk infecting your friends with whatever it is that you have? Do you want to put their lives in danger? Do you have any idea of the horrific images that swept through my mind when you were gripping my hand and wouldn't let go of it?"

Despair swept over Crawley's face, followed by resignation. "I guess you're right."

"I know I'm right, Mr. Crawley."

"Jon, please."

"Jon, if I've learned one thing from all my paranormal investigations, from my psychic ability, it's to trust my instincts. Every time I've ignored them, something has gone terribly wrong." She rubbed her brow. "Jon, can you remember when you first noticed these dark moods?"

He paused and rolled his eyes. "I think it happened after I was scratched by a cat in the bush a few weeks ago."

"Have you been to the doctor?"

"Yeah. I had all the tetanus shots. The doctor says I'm fine."

"That's a physician?"

"Yeah."

"What about a psychologist?"

"I go to a grief counseling group once a week, but I don't see a psychologist."

Kathleen sensed this was beyond a psychologist's area of expertise. But she didn't know what else to say to this troubled man. She had hung out her shingle only six months ago—after her previous job of teaching children with autism had become too stressful—but she usually knew what to tell her customers. Either she would have no visions, or she would have very clear visions, which would allow her to describe the images and interpret them in a helpful way. But this case was different. There was some dark and evil presence in this man's body, and the dark energy had, at least for a few seconds, permeated her body, filling her with powerful and explosive rage.

She knew eventually this grieving man would succumb to this rage. It wasn't a question of if. It was a question of when. And when he did, the results would not be pretty. She tried to muster a calm demeanor, although trembling hands refused to obey brain commands.

She stood up, providing a hint for her customer to follow suit. He did. "Listen, Jon. I would like you to go home and stay home until I call you, okay? I need some time to figure this out."

He slowly nodded and paid for the psychic reading. She thanked him, walked him to the door, said goodbye and closed it. But not before a cold blast of winter air swept into the small office. Kathleen shivered as she put her jacket on and got ready to leave.

But it was not from the cold air that she shivered.

Chapter Two

"It's cold out there," Jacob McCreery said a few hours later during a phone conversation with Kathleen. It usually was in the middle of November, and the winter of 2012 was no exception. The snow had begun to fall as soon as Kathleen left her office and made the short walk home. The weatherman had said gale force winds were expected overnight, along with an estimated 15 centimeters of snow. An ugly Atlantic storm was on its way. She felt alone and isolated when she got home. She greeted her faithful black cat, Spike, had a quick shower, ate dinner and reclined on the couch, the purring cat curled up on her lap.

That's when bad thoughts about Jon's visit had invaded her mind and she had to talk to someone. Who better than her loyal friend, Jacob, who had always been there for her when she needed a shoulder to cry on or some moral support? She and Jacob often commiserated. They had both lost their spouses, who were both victims of murder during paranormal investigations at around the same time. Kathleen and Jacob had grieved together, vented to one another, and slowly recovered from the tragic losses. Jacob had also been good friends with Mark, Kathleen good friends with Angela. Their joint nurturing fell just short of something more intimate.

There was a line they both refused to cross—although they had come close.

A few weeks ago, Kathleen had been thinking about Mark and all the things she had enjoyed doing with him. She called Jacob at about eleven in the evening, asking him to come over.

She needed him. So he had dutifully driven over and spent the night with Kathleen. In her bed.

They had hugged for a while, Kathleen cried a little, and then they had drifted off to sleep. Nothing happened. When Kathleen woke up, Jacob had already left. But there was a note:

> *Had a great time with you last night. Hope to see you soon. Remember, call me anytime if you need me. xx. Jake.*

It seemed that after that transgression, if you could call it that, the relationship had changed. Jacob had become more reserved and reluctant to put himself in a situation that might spiral out of control. But now she wanted him again, if for nothing else than to talk, tell him her fears about Jon, get his opinion. Two heads were always better than one. *Is that all I want him for?*

She didn't know. There was something about that night they had spent together. For a split second, she had felt like someone else. She couldn't explain why she suddenly wanted him in a hotly passionate way. But she did know that now was probably not the time or the place to be thinking about it.

"I know it's cold," she said. "But I need to talk to you. And I don't want to do it over the phone." She glanced at the wall clock. Hell, it was only 7:36 pm, not as bad as the timing of her last invite. She hoped he would agree. He usually did.

There was a pause before Jacob said: "Give me five minutes." He only lived a few blocks away. "Actually, there's something I want to tell you."

Kathleen only had a few minutes to think about what it might be. She wasn't able to figure it out by the time she heard a knock on the door. Jacob—short brown hair, two-day stubble, black-framed glasses and green eyes—smiled as she let him in. He wasn't bad looking.

Kathleen had been told she wasn't a bad-looking woman either.

A few minutes later they sat on the couch with hot mugs of tea. Kathleen used to drink coffee, but her doctor told her herbal tea was far less likely to cause anxiety attacks, which, a few months ago, had become an unwelcome addition to her life. Thanks initially to medication and now to the efforts of her counselor, Betty Shifert (Jacob jokingly called her Betty Shit-fer-brains, although she had helped him through his initial grieving period after the loss of Angela), Kathleen had finally been able to manage the anxiety attacks. They were far less of an unwelcome intrusion than they had been.

Jacob cupped his mug of caffeinated black tea while Kathleen sipped lemon herbal tea and explained what had happened with Jon. The wind began howling outside as the snowstorm intensified.

"The whole thing freaked me out," she said. "And the rage I felt, I can't explain it. I've never felt a pent-up violence like that before."

The color had been slowly draining from Jacob's face as she told the story, and now it was as pale as the falling snow. "So Jon's at home now?"

"I hope so. That's what I told him to do. You have any ideas?"

"You've thought of Detective Redmond?"

"Yes, I have. I wanted your opinion. Do you think we should call him?" As soon as she said it, Kathleen realized just how stupid it sounded. How many terrifying paranormal events had Detective Redmond bailed them out of in the past? And she knew damn well if she didn't call him, something terrible did happen, and he found out she knew and could have prevented it, there would be hell to pay. The detective was a good friend. But he also had a bad temper and didn't put up with bullshit from anyone—especially his friends.

"It seems obvious to me," Jacob said.

Noticing a seductive look from Jacob she had never seen directed at her before, Kathleen picked up the phone and speed-dialed the Redmond. One ring and his gruff voice responded. It softened when he recognized Kathleen. Either he had been napping or just not watching his call display. She felt just the tiniest trickle of panic as she rushed through the story, finishing with, "I think it might be a good idea to drive by his house and make sure he *is* home."

"Is this another story that's going to turn into a fucking nightmare?" the detective asked.

"I don't know." But that wasn't quite true. She did know. But, she hoped, against all historical odds, that this one time her gut instinct would be wrong.

"I think you do know," Redmond said. "But I'll go by and call you in the morning, okay?"

"Perfect." She hung up.

Trying to quash her sense of dread, she turned to Jacob, who was staring at her with concern. He knew her well enough to know when she was scared. He had seen the expression more times than he cared to remember.

"Now what was it you wanted to tell me?" she said.

Chapter Three

"Tell me you'll be back tonight?" Jeanette said as Redmond pulled his thick blue parka on, preparing to face the nasty storm.

"I'll be back tonight," he said reassuringly as he inserted his gun into shoulder-strapped holster strapped and verified that his belt holster also contained a firearm. When it came to leads from Kathleen Freeborne, Blaine Redmond knew only too well to arrive armed—well armed. He wasn't about to leave anything to chance.

"Jon lives a few blocks away. I'm just going to go check on him and then I'm coming right home." He kissed his wife and headed for the door. Then he turned around. "Honey, I forgot my smokes on the kitchen table. Could you grab them, please?"

Jeanette stifled a grimace. Her husband had given up alcohol, but had yet to give up the dreaded cigars. But she wasn't about to give him a hard time right now either. For all she knew, it would be the last time she would ever see her man alive. And she certainly didn't want him to leave on a bad note—whining at him to kick the nasty habit. He wasn't perfect, but he had become a good and caring husband. He had stopped the boozing and, after almost dying in the line of duty recently, had precipitously taken a renewed interest in their relationship. Not everything had improved, but many things had. And she had known when she married him that it was it was a sacrifice she had to make—that the stress might get to him and he might pick up some nasty habits. *Maybe he's a smoker now. But still much better than having him slobbering drunk, completely ignoring me. So, if nothing else, make the goodbyes positive and memorable.*

She returned with the package of cigars and handed them to Redmond. On an impulse she hugged him tightly and pressed her lips to his. "You smell good," he said, winking. "Trust me, I won't be gone long."

"I love you."

"I love you." He closed the door and headed out into the winter storm.

What should have been a five-minute drive took Redmond fifteen. The side streets were icy, visibility poor. The snow froze as it hit the windshield and at one point he had to pull over, swearing and cursing, to take a scraper to the windshield and manually free the wipers, which had frozen stuck.

He arrived at Jon's home just as the wipers began clunking, on the verge of freezing motionless again. "Damn storm," he said, exiting the unmarked patrol car. "Why didn't I settle down in the Caribbean?"

He noticed there was no porch light on as he covered his face with his arm and walked up the small sidewalk leading to Jon's house. *That's odd. He always keeps that light on, even when he's out at night, which isn't very often.*

Redmond started to get a little more concerned after he rang the doorbell three times and no one answered. Jon was one of the regulars he occasionally had coffee with at the local Tim Hortons, and he hoped he wasn't in any kind of trouble. Redmond knew he could have just called Jon, but, after what Kathleen had said, he wanted to see the man in the flesh. His detective instincts would be able to tell him if something was wrong. A phone call might not.

Three more rings.

Nothing.

He knocked hard on the door. Still nothing. He pulled out his phone, dialed Jon's number and listened to the phone ring over and over. No answer. He tried the door. It was locked. He decided to try the back door. He walked alongside the house and opened the small wooden gate to the yard. As it creaked, a black cat hissed, glaring with yellow eyes, and darted away.

Redmond felt his heartbeat quicken. *Calm yourself, for fuck sakes.*

He walked up the steps of the small porch. A small candle faintly illuminated the rear kitchen. He scanned the room through the window.

Then he froze.

Jonathon Crawley sat on a wooden chair at the kitchen table, holding a 12-gauge shotgun to his chin.

"Jon, no!" Redmond yelled, kicking the door open and rushing into the kitchen. "Jon, please get that shotgun away from your head."

Jon smiled at him without moving the shotgun or releasing his fingers from the trigger. Then the smile slowly faded. "It's my time. Take a step and I pull the trigger. Don't, and I pull the trigger ... you don't have a lot of choices, do you?"

"Jon, buddy. Don't ... please. I'll help you. It's not that bad. It's never that bad. Jon ... please!! I've been to the abyss and I've crawled my way out. You can, too."

"No I can't," Jon said resolutely, and pulled the trigger, bits of skull, skin, blood and brain matter splattering kitchen cabinets.

Chapter Four

My brain isn't working, Jacob thought as he walked in total darkness, wondering where he was. *This must be a dream.* But there was an eerily real quality about it. He didn't know if he was on another plane of existence, if he had actually been transported to this dark place. *Maybe I'm sleeping at home, completely enveloped by the black cloud,* the term he used to describe his depression when it surfaced and debilitated his mind. But, through counseling, and with the help of Betty Shit-fer-brains and Kathleen, he was doing an admirable job of keeping the black cloud at bay. Naturally he was still grieving over the tragic loss of Angela, the woman he had planned on marrying one day, and her smiling face still haunted him occasionally. But he was getting through the grieving process and on the mend.

Except now he was enveloped in darkness and had no idea where he was. So he stumbled along, feeling along cold stone walls for directions.

Then he saw it. A small yellow light, way off in the distance, somewhere at the end of what he could now discern was a winding corridor, a tunnel of sorts. He removed his hands from the cold walls, now guided by the diffuse light, and continued to walk.

He stopped momentarily and looked behind him. Total blackness. He felt a thin line of cold start at his lower back, crawl up his spine, and settle at the nape of his neck. He shuddered.

He continued walking, wiping the cold spot with his right hand, hoping to erase its frigid hold. It lingered for a few seconds before shooting into his brain, accompanied by a stab of pain like brain-freeze from gulping a Slurpee too fast. He grimaced, closed his eyes, and stopped, waiting for his brain to thaw. A short time later, it did and he carried on, the light ahead growing brighter.

He reached a candle-lit opening with a king-sized bed in the middle of the cavernous room. The bed was decorated in deep red satin linens and a nude woman, concealed partly by the richly textured blankets, slept in a fetal position, her back to Jacob.

That looks like Angela, he thought as he approached the bed. Then he saw the face. Beautiful and calm. Sleeping beauty. It was Angela.

He felt a wave of affection as he sat down beside her. He felt something else, too: the stirrings of sexual desire. How long had it been? Five, six months, maybe? He put his hand on her shoulder and the blanket slipped away, a firm breast revealing itself. God, those breasts looked inviting. Those blue eyes so captivating.

She opened her eyes. "Jacob. I knew you'd come. I've been waiting."

"Angela, is it really you?"

"Yes, sweetie, I'm here. I want you."

He bent down and kissed her full and passionately on the lips, letting his tongue linger in her mouth, explore, taste, savor the love of his life. He didn't want it to end. If it was a dream, he didn't want to wake up.

She removed her lips, reclined on her back, and spread her arms wide in an inviting gesture. She smiled—that crooked smile that drove him crazy. Her nipples had grown erect and her luscious breasts defied gravity.

She caught his glance and winked. "Make love to me baby. Fuck me ... please." She moaned softly.

He stripped off his sweatpants and t-shirt, climbed into bed and began kissing her, letting his hands roam freely over the body he knew so well, and missed so much.

The pleasure of the union was intense and satisfying. He reached another level, another plane of bliss and euphoria. A world where nothing else mattered but this union—no thoughts were permitted to interrupt this carnal enjoyment. He was riding high above the Earth on a white cloud of bliss, together with the woman of his dreams—perhaps in his dreams, he didn't know—but it felt so right, so real, so intensely pleasurable.

Reaching a powerful climax, he shuddered and moaned along with Angela as wave after wave of pleasure shook him to the very core of his soul. He had no idea lovemaking could be this intensely fulfilling. The waves gently subsided, the waters calmed and his heartbeat slowed. He listened to it now, still wrapped in a tight embrace with the object of his desire. *Please don't let this end ... please don't let this end. I want my Angela back.*

"Hey sleepy head, you want some tea?"

Jacob slowly opened his eyes, blinked a few times, and the recognition of where he was, whose voice it was, dawned on him. "Kathleen?"

"Of course it's me," she said, setting the tray on the bed. She wore a long sheer white nightgown that accentuated her slender frame. "Who did you expect? Snow White? An angel from heaven?"

"How about an Angela from heaven," he said, wiping sleepy eyes and reaching for a hot cup of tea.

"Did you dream of her last night?"

"Yes." He noticed his clothes and boxers were on the floor, the blankets crumpled. A white sheet barely concealed his naked body. *I never sleep in the nude. What happened?*

"Must have been a good one," Kathleen said, looking at the disheveled bed, the clothes strewn haphazardly on the floor.

She had made sure to prepare the guest bedroom for him, not wanting a repeat of the night a few weeks back, a night that seemed to distill the intimacy they had established.

But something strange had happened last night and she woke up soaked in sweat, a pleasurable sensation still permeating her body. There was a dream. Or was it a dream? Kathleen didn't know, but she felt her actions had been guided by Angela. That Angela had actually been inside of her body—spirit attachment or possession, whatever you wanted to call it. But the woman's intentions were absent of malice. She wanted a union with her man. She didn't intend her best friend any harm. She just wanted to borrow Kathleen's body and mind and have a carnal episode with Jacob. Nothing wrong with that, right? Kathleen wasn't so sure. The whole thing—if her instincts were accurate—was starting to sound awfully creepy.

They exchanged puzzled glances.

Noticing Jacob's embarrassed and confused expression, she turned to leave. "I'll let you sort yourself out."

About twenty minutes later, he had showered and dressed and was on the way out the door. Sitting at the kitchen table in her nightgown, Kathleen marveled at how fast he could get ready, the towel-dry brush cut certainly an asset in that regard.

He stood at the door, cheeks flushed pink with embarrassment. Had anything actually happened? If he had slept with her, he thought he was sleeping with Angela. And, during that blank space, Kathleen suspected that she had actually become Angela. The doubts lingered.

But the news last night had reinforced her suspicions. Hadn't he told her that sometimes when he looked at her, her expressions, even the sound of her voice, seemed to take on the characteristics of his deceased girlfriend? Yes, he had. *I've heard the voices myself. How many times? Twice maybe. Were they real? Or am I cracking up?*

"I have to get some work done," Jacob said, breaking the uncomfortable silence. "Are you going into work?"

"I have an appointment in the afternoon."

"Thanks for everything." He blushed at his choice of words. "I'll call you later. Let me know what you find out from Redmond." He closed the door behind him.

The phone rang a minute after Jacob left. She frowned, picked it up, the anticipatory dread tightening in her stomach.

"It isn't good," Redmond said.

He didn't have to say it. Kathleen already knew. "Jon?"

"He's dead. Blew his brains out with a shotgun. Do you have time for a coffee?"

"The usual haunt?" She did not intend the pun.

"Yeah. Will an hour from now work?"

Kathleen agreed and hung up. In the course of twenty-four hours she had already slept with one of her best friends and one of her clients had blown his brains out.

The day wasn't starting off well. Maybe a talk with Redmond would help?

Chapter Five

While Redmond talked, Kathleen distractedly watched four teenagers playing with their smartphones at a nearby table. Kathleen was a good multi-tasker and she could often follow multiple conversations simultaneously.

Redmond spoke in whispered tones, cognizant of the crowd. The small coffee shop was packed full of patrons and a line of people stood waiting for their afternoon caffeine jolts.

"I need a new fucking phone," the black-haired female teenager said. She was dressed in black goth. A black tattoo on her partially nude shoulder said: *If there is no belief, there is nothing.*

"That's a fucking piece of shit," said a long-haired boy sitting across from her. He held up a white iPhone. "You should get one of these."

The goth chick nodded and busied herself texting. The other three went back to texting, watching videos, playing games, or whatever the hell people do with smartphones. Every once in a while, one of them would display the screen from a phone and the others would look at it and laugh. In between eating and texting, the reveal-your-cell-phone-screen ritual continued.

Kathleen couldn't help but think how much the technological revolution had changed the fabric of culture. These kids couldn't be any older than sixteen, yet they couldn't sit down and eat lunch together without constantly entertaining themselves with their phones. Their lives revolved around their phones. They seemed more enamored with the phones than with each other. She wondered how many friends they had on Facebook, how many of them were really their friends, and how many hours a day they spent on the social networking site, living a vicarious life through other "friends" trivial and mindless status updates.

Remembering George Orwell's dystopian novel *1984,* in which he talked about an age when information was controlled by Big Brother and monitored by the Thought Police, she couldn't help but think just how prophetic his words were. *Is anything private anymore?* she wondered, recalling a story her girlfriend Anne Gruneld had told her about how governments, banks, and police all monitor Facebook, checking in on the users, determining their spending habits, personalities, favorite things to say and do, everything they've liked and tagged. And, she believed, Facebook wouldn't hesitate to sell the information to anyone willing to pay for it. Hell, they were probably selling it already.

Anne, who was an adamant anti-Facebooker (she called it Facefuck) had been quick to criticize the world's biggest social network for successfully making personal and private details public. And she steadfastly refused to get involved. She had even relayed a story to Kathleen that she had received a flyer in the mail from a service station she did not care to disclose, offering a free oil change in exchange for the coupon. When Anne brought the coupon into the station, the bright-eyed front desk attendant said, "Sure, we'll honor it. All you have to do is like us on Facebook."

To which Anne had responded: "I don't have a Facebook account."

But the young man had an answer. "There's a computer in the back, go ahead and sign one up."

Enraged, Anne stormed out of the station.

The goth chick revealed her phone screen to the inquisitive eyes of her friends. "Look what Tyler just posted on Facebook. He's taking a shit right now."

The table of four lit up in uncontrollable laughter.

Redmond cast the group an annoyed look. He didn't have a lot of patience for the younger generation, particularly those who walked around in broad daylight looking like vampires, swearing and fiddling with their smartphones all day. Smartphones, stupid users. *But was it just the kids?* he wondered. It seemed like everybody had smartphones these days, carried them wherever they went, and wanted to stay connected. At least he had the courtesy to leave his phone in the car when he conversed. He noticed, with a ray of hope, that Kathleen must have left hers at home. Yet it seemed very few people took any time out of their connected lives to actually slow down and smell the roses.

It didn't matter. He had finished his story and asked Kathleen if she wanted to see the inside of Jon's house, maybe get a feel for what caused his violent suicide.

She paused, distracted by the uproar at the table in front of her.

"Did you hear me?" he asked, taking a sip of coffee. Usually clean-cut, Redmond sported a two-day growth and looked a little grizzled. His eyes gave revealed he was worried about something, a little out of sorts. Kathleen decided she wouldn't ask. Not yet anyway.

"I heard you. I have a palm reading at three. Can we go now?"

"Sure," he said, rolling his eyes at the cackling teens. "Fucking technology. It'll be the bane of our existence. You watch."

"Do you have a Facebook account?" she asked.

"Yeah, but it's for investigative purposes only. Do you?"

Kathleen knew Redmond probably already knew the answer, but she decided to humor him. "Yeah, but I hardly use it. Mainly for family connections. I don't trust it."

"You shouldn't," Redmond said knowingly as they exited the coffee shop.

Kathleen was glad to get out of there; the noise level becoming much too loud for her sensitive ears. She didn't go in for a lot of loud talking unless she was drunk. And she didn't get drunk that often.

They drove the short distance to Jon's house through snow-covered streets. The storm had ended, but not before blanketing the tiny island with about 15 centimeters of snow. The weatherman had gotten it right for a change. The sun shone brightly but otherwise it was a cold, crisp day. Snow plows were busy clearing the white-blanketed roads.

They pulled up in front of the house. One marked and one unmarked cop car were parked outside. There was still investigating going on.

"Did Jon say anything to you about a cat?" Redmond asked as they went up the walkway, careful to step in the deep footprints created by current and previous visitors.

Kathleen nodded. "He said he noticed his dark mood swings just after getting scratched by a black cat a few weeks back."

"Did he say where?"

"In the forest somewhere. I didn't ask. The rage that boiled through me when I touched him was ... well, it was hard to take. I was a little out of sorts." For the first time, Kathleen thought of her cat and hoped she wouldn't be implicated. Spike had been known to wander off for days at a time. "Why?"

"I saw a black cat on the property, just before I saw Jon."

Kathleen inhaled deeply and let out a slow breath. She knew Spike was home last night. Good. She had an alibi—at least for last night. Who knew about a few weeks ago?

"What's all this?" Kathleen asked as they surveyed the kitchen where the suicide occurred. The body had been removed, but the area was cordoned off with yellow crime scene tape. There was blood and brain matter splattered around and two forensics experts were swabbing at the gooey mess. There was a cop in the living room sifting through personal possessions, and Kathleen heard footsteps upstairs—probably of a fourth investigator rummaging around.

"Just a formality," Redmond said after acknowledging the others. "The medical examiner is going to do an autopsy. Among other things, we have to determine what kind of meds Jon might have been taking. And crime lab is doing a sweep. Are you feeling anything?"

"Not yet," Kathleen said, walking into the living room while Redmond talked to an official in the kitchen.

Police Detective Russ Willard was flipping through some mail on a coffee table in the tidy, sparsely furnished room.

He smiled at Kathleen warmly. "How's our resident psychic doing?" They had become friends a few months back during the Poison Rage case.

She smiled at the clean-cut detective. "Don't want to complain. No one likes listening to a whiner anyway."

"That's true enough," Willard said, examining a stack of unopened mail.

Kathleen sat down in an old brown leather Lazy Boy chair in front of the television set, hoping to calm her mind enough to pick up a vibe. So far she was registering nothing, other than the dark feeling of death that usually surfaced under these circumstances. She closed her eyes, searching for an image, knowing if it was there it would come. She didn't always like being a psychic—sometimes she thought of her gift as psychotic—but she had decided to embrace it. After all, she earned a respectable living at it.

Willard ignored her and continued going about his business.

After a moment, she opened her eyes, stood up and decided to go upstairs. She wasn't getting a vibe. "Anything exciting in the mail?" she asked Willard, ascending the squeaky staircase. He had stopped rifling through the pile and was staring at an envelope. She didn't expect him to make her privy to a police investigation, but it didn't hurt to ask. After all, it was clearly a suicide anyway.

He glanced up, seeming a bit disturbed. "The usual, you know, bills and stuff. I don't think I'll find anything. This case is cut and dried." He smiled in an oddly affectionate way.

Kathleen nodded and proceeded up the stairs. She couldn't help noticing he had placed one of the envelopes aside and his expression told her something other than his words. *He's hiding something.*

But she didn't give it a second thought. Her mind was still trying to digest Jon's sudden suicide so soon after the psychic reading. She reached the landing and walked into the master bedroom. Reggie Snyden, a young uniformed cop, was going through the dresser drawers as she entered. A mischievous grin countenanced his boyish features. He had short-cropped black hair and brown eyes. Kathleen knew him casually. He was a skeptic of her powers.

He sang: "You gotta feeling ... a feeling deep inside, oh yeah."

That was the thing about being a psychic. You had to put up with the ridicule along with the praise. Kathleen had some idea of what it must be like to be a celebrity and it was not something she envied. There was no point in justifying the snide comment (or was that Snyden comment?) with a response, so she ignored it and glanced around the room.

Other than the mess Snyden was making, tossing clothing on the floor, the room was sparsely furnished and minimalist. The queen-sized bed was made and two bedside tables with decorative '60s lamps ornamented either side. A floral-patterned armchair sat in the corner and an antique wooden dresser with a decorative mirror stood against one wall. The drawers had been pulled open by Snyden and clothing was scattered on the finished oak hardwood floors. The walls were painted a light beige color, and two large windows with white Venetian blinds faced the quiet residential street outside.

Crawley obviously wasn't into collecting memorabilia. There was a single picture of him with his deceased wife displayed on a bedside table. Kathleen picked it up and studied it. It was a photo of the two, arm-in-arm, standing in front of their house on a bright, sunny day, staring at each other with love in their eyes. They appeared to be in their thirties. A white banner with black lettering hung over the front porch. In large and neatly printed capital letters, it read: *WELCOME HOME.*

We live and we die, Kathleen thought. *So finite. But there is another side, isn't there? I've seen it. I see it regularly. At least Jon has joined his wife and maybe now he's happy.*

Snyden snapped her out of the reflection and she carefully set the picture down.

"A feeling deep inside, oh yeah," he sang.

"I wish you would show more respect for the dead," she said, losing patience with his sarcastic humor. She was about to ask him if he would be so flippant if it was his father who had just blown his brains out with a shotgun, but bit her tongue. She didn't want to get in the bad books with cops. She didn't know when she might need them.

"Soooorrrrry," Snyden said. "Excuuuuuuuse me!"

It didn't matter. She wasn't getting a vibe anyway. It was time to leave. "No problem," she said, heading to the door. She accidentally kicked something and looked down at the floor. It was a gold necklace with a crucifix. Following her eyes, Snyden bent down and picked it up with a gloved hand. He dangled it in front of her. "Getting any vibe?"

"No. I usually have to touch something and I don't want to contaminate your evidence."

Snyden was only a few months into his police career and he came into it with an attitude typical of his generation. He thought he knew it all. But, other than stories, which he didn't believe, he knew nothing of the carnage and bloodshed that Kathleen had witnessed.

"Here," he said, handing it to her. "This is an open and shut case anyway. I don't see how this little necklace could possibly contribute anything to our investigation, if you want to call it that."

Kathleen took the necklace and examined it. It wasn't a crucifix at all, but a sword; a tiny replica of the same sword that had purged the town of the destructive evil force that had permeated its otherwise peaceful streets only a few months ago. She knew the actual sword, an ancient artifact that had been used in religious battles centuries ago, had been displayed at the haunted King's Playhouse Theatre for a time before being relocated to a museum in Halifax. But she had never seen a tiny replica of it. And what was Jon doing with it? Did he sense some impending evil and hoped the necklace would ward it off? And where did it come from? Who was making it and why? She thought the deadly evil had left PEI. Was it back?

She didn't have time to analyze these questions as Redmond entered. "What you got there?"

She handed it to him and apologized for contaminating evidence. He resignedly shook his head and held it up with a gloved hand. His expression changed from curiosity to concern.

"What the fuck is with this mess?" he asked Snyden, who flinched. Snyden might make snide comments to some people, but he respected and revered the seasoned detective.

ll do is clean this shit up and leave it how
dmond said, his eyes darkening. "Jon's family
ɔm Halifax tomorrow to deal with his estate.
And I dc. ant them thinking the cops here are a bunch of
fucking inept and disrespectful slobs. You got that?"

Snyden nodded, his face reddening.

"I'll deal with this," Redmond said, slipping the necklace
into an evidence bag. "You know better than that, Kathleen,"
he scolded.

"Sorry."

A few minutes later, Redmond drove her to Tim Hortons
parking lot, where her Camry was parked.

Midway through the short trip, his anger diffused. He
asked her about vibes, to which she shook her head. He made
her promise to call him if she received any visions that might
explain why Jon had suddenly decided to end his life, and
promised to update her on the origin and purpose of the
mysterious necklace. Redmond wasn't happy that Kathleen
had potentially contaminated important evidence. But he
wasn't stupid enough to alienate her either. He knew only too
well her psychic intuition had benefited previous investigations
immensely.

Her eyes were downcast as he pulled up beside the Camry.

She wasn't looking forward to her afternoon reading. Her
last customer had died, her best friend Angela seemed to have
unlimited visitation rights to her body and mind, Jacob was
behaving oddly since the passionate night, and something was
not quite right on the island anymore. She could feel the faint

tingling of the edge creeping back into her mind. *Can thing any worse?* But she already knew the answer.

"Are you okay?" Redmond asked as she exited the vehicle.

She hadn't told the detective all her problems. The thing about Angela was just too creepy. But there was no point in lying, either. "No, I'm not."

"Hang in there, kid," he said. "Call me if you need anything."

"Thanks," she said, trying on a smile and not quite managing it. "Again, sorry about the necklace."

"It's behind us. What's behind is not important."

She thought the statement was only partially true as she started her Camry and pulled out of the parking lot. It was a generalization, after all. And weren't generalizations, by their very nature, only half truths?

Sometimes, what's behind you is extremely important.

Chapter Six

"I tried to put it behind me," Lori Bellafonte said as she took a seat at the reading table in Kathleen's small office. "But it keeps cropping up in my mind. I need to do something about it."

Lori was 36, almost six feet tall, medium build, with an olive complexion, long, flowing brown hair and bright brown eyes. The whites of her eyes were stunningly white, matching her perfect teeth. The combination spoke of excellent health. A disposition that was normally cheery had recently been marred by some unpleasantness. She had explained to Kathleen earlier on the phone that her husband, one Reggie Snyden, had for some unknown reason begun to distrust her lately. Lori worked as a corporate lawyer and her job description typically called for her to entertain corporate clients over dinner and drinks at fancy restaurants. She had been making inroads into landing a large contract with a casino company that wanted to open a big casino on the island. Casinos Inc. was looking into a structure as a foundation that would effectively lower the amount of income tax it was paying.

Lori had wooed CEO Sid Ballis by extolling the tax benefits of the new structure as well as locating a casino site in a choice location in Charlottetown. She had also gone to great lengths with some preliminary applications to various federal, provincial, and local authorities. And, while she had yet to sign a lengthy and lucrative contract with Casinos Inc., she had been put on retainer and was billing out big bucks.

Reggie, it seemed, had become jealous of the time Lori had been putting into her work and had also suspected her relationship with Sid was more than just business. Over the past few weeks, their relationship had started to deteriorate. The intimacy and deep connection they once shared were fast becoming a fading memory.

"I do think you need to do something," Kathleen said. "We need to get some preliminary things out of the way first." She remembered Snyden's snide comments and was beginning to understand a little better what might be upsetting the young cop. "Does Reggie know you're here?"

"Oh no. He frowns on this kind of stuff."

"Not to worry," Kathleen said, opening a small drawer and pulling out some forms. "I take client confidentiality seriously." She slid the forms across the table. "I require you to sign these before we begin. They're disclaimers, absolving me of responsibility should something go—ah ... wrong. They indicate your participation in this session is at your own risk, that I will keep everything you tell me strictly confidential. The only exception is if the information you give me might carry some weight in a criminal investigation. In other words, if disclosing information about our session might lead to the arrest and incarceration of a serial killer, this gives me permission to divulge it. I couldn't sleep at night if I found out I had information that I knowingly withheld that might have saved lives had it been released. I hope you're okay with that? You're a lawyer, so you should understand."

Lori paused as her legal mind processed the information. "Has that ever happened?"

Kathleen thought about the information about Jon Crawley she had divulged. She didn't know if it qualified.

"Maybe once. But that's an ongoing investigation that I'm not at liberty to discuss."

Lori took a few minutes to read the forms, scribbled her signature, and pushed them back in front of Kathleen, who put them neatly in the drawer. "All right, we're ready to begin."

Taking Lori's hand, she said: "Please close your eyes and try to blank your mind."

They joined hands. Lori closed her eyes and Kathleen followed suit.

She brought herself to a rushing river. She was on an inflatable boat, barreling down the river, the waves floating the craft on a zigzagging course as it snaked its way down. The steep incline of the river slowly changed, the angle gradually transforming into a gentler and more manageable slope. The whites of the waves shrank in their ferocity until finally the small boat drifted into calm waters, Lori and Kathleen clutching the side ropes for support. They were in a large lake, calm, pale blue, surrounded by lush green mountains, deep blue sky and popcorn clouds.

They drifted out to the middle of the lake, slowly released their tight grips on the ropes, and floated to a gentle stop. If Kathleen was to have any visions, it was right here in this calm, otherworldly place that they would become apparent.

She slowly settled into a meditative trance, all her problems vanishing—a singular focus on the plight of her client. The face of Reggie Snyden came into focus, emerging from above in one of the clouds. And another face in another cloud. It was Russ Willard, her friend who had recently been promoted to detective.

They were having a conversation about Lori.

"What's your problem?" Willard said.

"I don't know. She isn't around much lately."

"What do you expect? She's a corporate lawyer, trying to land a big contract. That takes time, effort and some schmoozing. It's the nature of the beast."

"I think her interest in Sid is more than just business."

"How do you know that?"

"I don't. I just think it. I've seen the way he looks at her."

"Does she reciprocate?"

"I don't know."

"Has she ever fooled around before?"

"I don't think so."

"Maybe you're jealous of her success? A lot of men are. Not me, but a lot of men."

"Could you do me a favor?" Snyden asked.

"What's that?" Willard said.

"Keep an eye on her."

"I don't know."

"I'll pay you."

"I don't know."

The images slowly faded, the conversation cut short. Kathleen was abruptly transported to The Pilot House in Charlottetown, a popular restaurant and bar.

Lori and Sid sat across from each other, discussing business. Dinner plates containing leftovers sat next to them. They both sipped pints of beer. Sid was a hulk of a man, with chiseled features and black hair tied back neatly in a ponytail. He smiled at Lori while he sipped beer. "We are certainly considering signing with you, but we need more time."

"Time for what? I've been on retainer for three months. You can see I know what I'm doing. This new foundation structure will save you hundreds of thousands of dollars a year in income tax payments. And it's all legal, above board."

"I know."

"And don't forget about the applications I've submitted on your behalf. We already got the green light at the local level, thanks to my contacts at city hall."

"You've done an admirable job. I was just hoping our relationship could ... I don't know ... evolve a little beyond the business realm."

Lori straightened in her seat. She removed her hand from the Kokanee Gold draft, looked Sid straight in the eye. "I'm not willing to compromise my morals over business. I'm married."

The image faded and soon Kathleen was looking again at the popcorn clouds. Then another violent image appeared in the clouds above. She knew instinctively this was not an image of what was behind. No. It was an image of what was ahead. Though not necessarily what would be. Kathleen had discovered if you change your actions, you can indeed change the course of your destiny and change the future. It was an image of what could be, but also could be altered.

Lori and Reggie argued vehemently, throwing objects around their upscale condo in downtown Charlottetown. "I want you to get the fuck out of this apartment now," Snyden said, pointing to the door. "Get your shit and leave."

"What are you talking about? I paid for this place before we met. You leave."

He stepped forward, fists raised in fury. Lori grabbed her high-heel shoe and flung it at him. He ducked and it smashed a window. The crashing glass brought a momentary silence to their battle.

Lori jerked her hands free, opened her eyes, and stared at Kathleen.

Kathleen heard the sound of breaking glass as if it was right in her office. She opened her eyes and realized it was. Caught up in the vision, she had knocked over a glass of water with her elbow and it had shattered into a million pieces on the wooden floor.

She blinked a few times, registering the visions, processing the information, trying to decide how she would advise her client. She stalled for time. "Did you see or feel anything?"

"No," Lori said, glancing down at the shards of glass and spilled water. "But I heard something."

"Sorry about that." Kathleen got up, fetched a nearby broom and dustpan, cleaned the mess up and sat down. Lori was searching her eyes inquisitively.

"Well?" she asked. "Did you have any visions? Can you advise me?"

Kathleen nodded and took a few moments before answering. "Have you told Reggie about Sid?"

"What do you mean?" She squirmed in her seat, crossed her hands, and stared at Kathleen accusatorily.

"Don't get defensive. You came here for help. And that's what I'm trying to give you."

The lawyer's countenance softened. "He knows Sid's a client."

"Did you tell him that Sid propositioned you, that he wants to sleep with you?"

A hint of red emerged on Lori's cheeks. "No. Did you see that?"

"Yes, I did. Maybe Reggie's insecure or something, I don't know. Maybe he's even jealous of your success. Maybe he thinks he'll lose you. But you should tell him what Sid said and that you flatly refused him. Maybe he'll be upset but in the long run I think he'll appreciate your honesty. You haven't been together for that long, and I don't think it's good to keep secrets like that from your husband—especially since he's a cop. He could have you watched."

"Maybe you're right," Lori said after a short pause.

"And another thing. And this is an ethical thing that you might not agree with. I would have a talk with Sid and tell him in no uncertain terms that your relationship with him is strictly business. If he has a problem with that, you might want to consider dumping him as a client. If your marriage suffers if you continue the business relationship, you might want to ask yourself: Is the money worth it?"

"Thanks for that," Lori said. "Anything else?"

Kathleen knew she had to be extremely guarded in terms of how much information she released. Too much could be disastrous. Too little could also be disastrous. There was a fine line that she was very cognizant of. She had to get it just right if she planned on saving this woman's relationship.

"Let me ask you something. Do you love your husband?"

"Very much."

"Do you think you can be compatible long term?"

"I wouldn't have married him if I didn't."

"When was the last time you planned something special for him?"

"I don't know, maybe two months ago."

"Well, why don't you plan a romantic dinner? And do it soon. I think there's hope if you act quickly."

"Thank you. I'm going to take some of that advice."

Lori suspected that along with Kathleen's pearls of wisdom, there were some deliberate deletions. But, as a lawyer, she was also smart enough to realize that sometimes less was more.

Chapter Seven

Detective Redmond wanted more information, but it wasn't forthcoming. *Not right now, anyway,* he thought, sitting at his desk the following afternoon, jotting down notes. He had just gotten off the phone with forensic lab technician Stan Neiderman, and the short, middle-aged bald man had told him that there was a partial print on the gold necklace recovered at Jon's home, but nothing matched up in the crime database. They might have been able to find more had the evidence not been contaminated by an over-anxious Kathleen and Reggie Snyden, who had probably smeared any prints that might otherwise have been detectable.

But Redmond thought the clues to Jon's death would not necessarily be found on the necklace in the form of fingerprints, but rather in the origin of the piece of jewelry.

Neiderman had said the necklace was manufactured in China. A numbered company owned by Casinos Inc. had ordered thousands of them and they were being sold in jewelry stores in Halifax and Charlottetown.

What was interesting about the necklace was the ornate gold sword. At first glance, it could pass for a crucifix, but a closer look revealed it was actually an ancient sword, a tiny replica of the artifact that had been used to purge local residents of the violent evil force that had resulted in the deaths of about 104 residents in the recent past. Redmond knew that sword, after being used to bring law, order and sanity to the tiny island, was now on display in a museum in Halifax.

He puzzled over it. If someone was manufacturing and selling replicas of a sword used in the name of good, wouldn't the intention be to ward off evil spirits? If so, what was so wrong about that? But Jon hadn't been wearing the necklace when he died. Where did he get it? Why wasn't he wearing it? And why did he commit suicide? And why was Casinos Inc. involved in the production and distribution of it?

He looked down at his steno pad. He still preferred the traditional way of cultivating clues and solving puzzles. He wrote *sword necklace* on the pad and beside it a question mark. Below that he wrote *Hannah and Holly*, Jon's niece and daughter. They would be arriving tomorrow to arrange for a funeral. Or was it today? Perhaps they could shed some light on the necklace and Jon's mental state before he died.

He looked at the steno pad again and wrote *Sid Baillis.* He wanted to find out why a large casino company had such a keen interest in a small necklace. Something didn't smell right about that. He would have to question Sid and perhaps his corporate lawyer, Lori Bellafonte, whom he knew casually. He wrote her name down, and beside it wrote *Reggie Snyden*. Reggie was her husband. Maybe he could shed some light on things.

Finally, he wrote *black cat* with a question mark beside it. Kathleen had told him Jon had mentioned getting scratched by a black cat. Maybe it was worth combing the woods in search of this little feline. Never mind just the woods, the town of Montague as well. After all, Redmond had seen a black cat just prior to seeing Jon blow his brains out. Maybe it was just a coincidence that Jon had been scratched prior to his untimely end. Or maybe this feline had infected Jon with some rage virus. Maybe he had killed himself before this rage could become full blown and cause him to hurt or kill others? Maybe he knew he was infected and it was only a matter of time before he got out of control? Kathleen had said she felt a rage during the psychic reading with him. She had described it as among the most disturbing sensations she had ever felt in her life. Certainly not the worst. She was an experienced psychic, a former ghost hunter. But at least in the top five.

Lots of questions. Not a lot of answers.

He made his plan. He would notify the other detectives of his theory on the black cat, have them keep an eye open for such a stray and, as absurd as it sounded, try to capture it. *An All-Points-Bulletin on an infected feline. Great.*

He would visit Sid Baillis and Lori Bellafonte to see if they could shed light on the necklace.

He would drive by the Crawley residence and see if there was anyone to talk to.

And he would have another conversation with Kathleen, just to keep up-to-date on her gut instincts, which he found much more finely tuned than his own, although he hated to admit it. *But she's a psychic. That doesn't count.*

Oh, right. He also needed to have conversations with Snyden and Willard, get up to speed with their theories.

He busied himself with a few phone calls and emails. He was just about to leave his office when the phone rang. He answered.

"Boss, I have some more information for you." It was Stan Neiderman again.

"Go ahead."

"We're still working on the autopsy, but I have some preliminary findings on blood tests."

Redmond had instructed Neiderman to call him immediately with any new information, however minor it might seem to the forensics department. "What did you find?"

"This man had the beginning stages of some kind of viral infection."

"What kind of viral infection?"

"We don't know, boss. This virus is unlike anything I've ever seen."

"How so?"

"For one, it spreads rapidly."

"What does it cause?"

"We can't tell you that, boss. This man's dead. It looks like he contracted it a few days ago, probably from that scratch. It quickly spread to a third of his body."

"How communicable is it?"

"At this rate it looks like blood only. But we're not taking any chances. There is a possibility this thing could become airborne."

"Have you advised local and federal disease control agencies?"

"I have, sir."

"What're they saying?"

"For now they're adopting a wait-and-see attitude. This doesn't constitute an epidemic. They don't want the whole island thrown into an unnecessary panic. But they want that cat captured and put down."

"Keep me posted."

"You got it, boss."

Redmond put down the receiver, grabbed his jacket and left. He took some satisfaction in the knowledge he had already put out an All-Points-Bulletin on a possible infected feline. But not a lot.

What had really happened to Crawley?

Chapter Eight

Since Redmond couldn't remember when Holly and Hannah were due to arrive at the Crawley residence, he had decided to drive over to the house. He hoped investigators had taken the necessary precautions during the investigation at the residence and the subsequent cleanup. Officials could decide to quarantine everybody who had come into contact with Crawley. And he was nagged by the thought that he had potentially been exposed to Jon's blood and become infected. He held out his arms, looking for some tell-tale sign, like a red rash. His arms looked normal.

Tracing back the events, he couldn't remember putting himself in any danger of infection after the gunshot. Unless, when Jon's head exploded, a drop of blood had landed in his eye. But he didn't think that had happened. He was just being a little paranoid. And that was normal, given the circumstances. His years as a detective had taught him to be extremely careful when dealing with blood.

He pulled down a quiet residential street a few blocks from Crawley's and was stunned by what he saw.

An elderly man lay on the sidewalk on his back in a pool of blood, a large rock beside his crushed skull. Two youths, possibly in their early twenties, were feeding on him. What? Feeding on him? One young man was biting into the neck and another was chewing on the man's face.

Had it started already?

Redmond couldn't believe the macabre spectacle but he reacted quickly. He screeched to a stop, exited the vehicle, extracted his firearm and pointed it at the cannibals. "Stop right now. Put your hands in the air and freeze."

One man ignored the order and continued feeding on the victim's face.

The other stopped, stood up and acknowledged Redmond, a faraway and wild look in his eyes. His arms outstretched like a zombie—there was no other way to describe it—he stumbled toward Redmond, mumbling something unintelligible. He took slow, plodding steps toward the detective while his face contorted and twisted—pain-filled and dark expressions. His face, neck and green jacket were covered in blood, bits of flesh dangling from his gaping mouth. He was out of his mind.

A few neighbors had opened their front doors and were staring at the spectacle in horror. Some filmed it with their smartphones.

"Don't take another step," Redmond shouted. "Or I'll shoot." It was times like this when the seasoned detective wished he operated with a partner.

The man ignored the detective and plodded forward. He was unarmed. It was too late to call for backup and Redmond didn't want to shoot these men if he could help it. By the looks of their condition, it appeared they had no idea what they had just done. It was either some drug, or infected rage. Redmond didn't have time to figure out all the possibilities.

He pulled his police baton out, charged forward, and whacked his attacker hard across the head. It was a damned good shot. The man dropped with a thud, knocked unconscious.

Redmond quickly pulled his handcuffs out and approached the other man, who was still busy eating human flesh. He grabbed both the man's arms quickly, locking them behind his back and fastening the cuffs. He stood up and kicked the man onto his back. The man exposed his teeth, growled like a wolf and shifted his eyes madly. The same dark, chilling, tortured expression contorted his features, and he started moaning and writhing in the blood-stained snow.

Finally, Redmond called for backup.

Chapter Nine

"No need to get your back up, Spike," Kathleen said a few nights later as she reclined on the couch in front of the television. Old Man Winter had arrived with a blast, or at least another three feet of snow piled high outside.

Spike had been purring contentedly on the couch beside her when she went to pat her. Initially Spike had tilted her small head up to receive the affection but then, without warning, she had arched her back, hissed and darted off the couch, down the hall and into the kitchen. Kathleen couldn't be sure, but she thought the cat had been behaving more skittishly than usual lately.

The last few days at work were relatively uneventful: a few readings, but nothing as dramatic as the readings with Lori or Jon.

Something else was bothering her. Redmond had called and filled her in on the infected feline, and wanted her gut feeling.

But she had drawn a blank and had nothing to offer the detective. He had briefly mentioned the story about the grisly zombie attack and had cut the call rather abruptly, saying he had some urgent business to attend to. "Check *The Guardian*," he had said before hanging up. "It's all in there."

She had the paper sitting in front of her now. It had been sitting there for the last few hours, but she had been reluctant to read it. From the way Redmond had described the incident, she didn't know if she wanted to know.

Finally, her curiosity got the better of her and she picked up the folded newspaper:

Man Killed In Zombie-Like Cannibal Attack

And elderly man was killed Friday afternoon after two men allegedly attacked him in the street, crushed his skull, and began feeding on him like zombies.

Norton Simmons, 86, was killed while walking on Patrick Street in Montague at approximately 5:43 pm. His skull was crushed with a large rock and part of his face and neck were eaten.

Ron Saunders, 21, and Robert Stoker, 23, have been charged with second-degree murder in connection with the incident and are in custody, according to Police Detective Blaine Redmond.

Redmond was driving when he noticed the two men bent over Simmons, eating his neck and face, his skull crushed in and a large rock in the snow nearby. "I approached them, leveled my gun and ordered them to stop," Redmond said. "They ignored me. At that point Saunders started slowly walking toward me with his eyes glazed over like a zombie. He was muttering something incomprehensible, while Stoker continued his attack on Simmons."

According to Redmond, he was able to restrain the attackers and call for backup without firing a shot.

Redmond suspects Stoker and Saunders were under the influence of a drug called "bath salts," a synthetic drug that can cause anger, hallucinations, extreme paranoia and delusions. He added that it will be some time before toxicology reports can confirm his suspicions, but small quantities of "bath salts" were found on both of the accused.

"I've seen people on this drug before and it's highly dangerous," Redmond said. "An ex-addict told me while he was in its grip he had the darkest and most evil thoughts that he has ever experienced in his entire life.

"There have been many documented incidents of people in the United States attacking others violently, in some cases committing murder, while under the influence of this drug. They literally turn into zombies.

"Let this be a warning to all you young people thinking of trying it. Don't. It will destroy your life," Redmond added.

Kathleen shuddered, crumpled the newspaper, and threw it under the coffee table. The news was very troubling. But she felt some relief in the knowledge that these zombies probably weren't infected with what Redmond had termed the Rage Virus, a virus he believed had infected Jon Crawley prior to his suicide. Where did *it* come from?

Kathleen felt alone and anxious. She craved some company and thought about calling her friend Anne. Anne was always good for entertainment. And good company, too. One thing about Anne—you might not agree with a lot of her opinions, but she held them with conviction and passion. She would become animated while espousing here beliefs. Kathleen looked at the clock: 7:36 pm.

Wait a minute. I haven't talked to Jacob in a while. It seemed since their little indiscretion, if you could call it that, he had been giving her a wide berth, perhaps embarrassed he had gone so far with a friend. But Kathleen hadn't been herself while she was making love to him. She had been Angela. That was the strange part.

She picked up the phone. If nothing else, she told herself, at least to warn him about the Rage Virus. He answered on the first ring.

"Jacob, how are you?"

"Good, and you?" He was reserved.

"Honestly, I'm feeling a bit lonely." She filled him in on what Redmond had said about the Rage Virus. She warned Jacob to steer clear of black cats, excluding Spike obviously, and told him to be extra vigilant around angry people. They talked briefly about the horrific zombie murder a few short blocks away, and finally Kathleen cut to the chase.

"Do you want to come over and ... I don't know, watch a movie, or something?"

Jacob hesitated for a moment. "Sure, give me fifteen minutes."

"Okay." Kathleen hung up. She had showered after work and thrown on jeans and a sweater. At her psychic center, she often dressed in more formal business attire. If you wanted people to believe you when you predicted the future, at least you could do so wearing something more professional than jeans and a sweater. That was Kathleen's opinion, anyway.

She couldn't help but feel a little nervous at Jacob's impending arrival. She didn't want to admit it to herself, at least not right now anyway, but she did find him attractive. Physically, he wasn't hard to look at. Mentally, or morally, he possessed qualities she admired. Honesty and loyalty were traits she found hard to come by in men, her late common-law husband, Mark, excepted. It had been many months since his death and sometimes she still longed for his company. She hadn't had a single date since, unless you could call that thing with Jacob a date—and Kathleen wasn't counting that. She also knew Jacob had not dated. They had talked about it briefly and both admitted they weren't quite ready.

But Kathleen understood that at some point she would have to entertain the notion. After all, she was still young, and she knew many men considered her attractive. She had probably turned down six dates since Mark's death. She was smart enough not to go into another relationship while grieving and careful not to put herself in a situation where she would be bringing her baggage into someone else's life or comparing everything they did to Mark. She knew that kind of logic was flawed. Mark was one-of-a-kind, and nobody would ever measure up to him.

So she had waited patiently, trying to go through the stages of grieving slowly, waiting until she felt mentally ready to jump into a relationship that might start off as a roller-coaster ride but with any luck would convert to—not a tilt-a-whirl—not the bumper cars either, but maybe a merry-go-round. That was it, a merry-go-round. *Me and my soul mate riding horses, going round and round to the sound of pleasant music, holding hands and laughing. Madly in love.*

But wow, the thought was scary. She remembered the struggles that she and Mark had endured before they finally reached an area of comfort, trust, happiness, deep love and respect for one another. Deciding where and when to compromise and when to hold your ground. Which battles to engage in, which ones to refuse. Learning to pay attention to your partner, cultivate the love long after the infatuation period wears off. Finding the inner beauty in your partner as the years begin to take a toll on the physical beauty—that which the media seems to thrive on, the singular image of beauty associated with youth, smooth skin, thinness, that perfect figure, on and on. The image of beauty that has become so ingrained—probably most of it subconscious—in the heads of the male species, but probably not so much for females, Kathleen thought.

She sighed deeply. God, she missed Mark. If only she could resurrect him from the dead. Falling in love wasn't easy at all. In this day and age, it was a daunting prospect. The whole introspective exercise was making her feel sad.

Her doorbell rang, snapping her out of the reflection. *Be happy. Don't bring your friend down. He's got his own shit right now. The last thing he needs is yours.*

She opened the door and her jaw dropped. Mark stood there, smiling like it was the most perfectly natural and normal thing in the world for him to be standing at her door on that chilly Saturday evening.

"Well ... aren't you going to invite me in?"

Chapter Ten

Drake Bellows didn't invite a lot of people into to his ramshackle cabin in the forest near Murray Harbour and the Atlantic Ocean. In fact, he didn't invite anybody in. At seventy-five, Drake had completely withdrawn from society about five years ago—selling his house in Montague after his wife had suddenly died of a heart attack. With the $120,000, he had bought three acres of land, assembled belongings and tools he thought he would need, including an old gray Ford pick-up truck, and went about building himself a small cabin. It wasn't much, haphazardly constructed out of plywood and whatever other materials he found or chopped down. It was about the size of a small bedroom, perhaps 12 x 14 feet, but it was all he needed. It had a wood-burning stove, and he had built an outhouse about thirty feet from the primitive dwelling. He lived without electricity and trucked in water. He hunted, fished, and his expenses were low. He rarely spent more than $150 in any given month.

He sat at his wooden kitchen table now, rolling a cigarette from a Drum tobacco pouch. Rays of sunshine shone into the cabin from the two small windows, painting yellow lines across his weathered features. The woodstove crackled and popped, and the smell of burning pine scented the otherwise musty shack.

A skinned rabbit dangled outside the window, secured with binder twine—today's supper.

But for the popping of the fire, the only sounds Drake could hear were the steady drips of the snow melting, sliding down and off the corrugated tin roof—plip, plop, plip, plop.

He finished rolling his smoke, lit it with a Zippo lighter, which he preferred to a Bic disposable, inhaled deeply and coughed.

He had lots of wood, a roof over his head, dinner hanging outside, an abundance of water and warm clothes. What else does a man need? Maybe the company of another person, but Drake didn't have much interest in that. He preferred talking to the animals, the foxes, rabbits, birds, squirrels, whatever he encountered during his long hikes. He felt animals made more sense than humans. At least they kept their fucking mouths shut. In his humble opinion, whenever humans spoke, most of the time what spewed forth was verbal diarrhea. And he had no inclination to listen to shit.

His only friend, Jonathon Crawley, had just committed suicide, and even they hadn't been that close. Once a month, Crawley would make the short drive to Drake's acreage and the two would usually sit at the ocean and fish, drink a twelve-pack of beer, and commiserate. Crawley had been obsessed with the death of his wife, and if Drake had to be completely honest with himself, the one person he wished he still had in his lonely and reclusive existence was his late wife, Greta. He missed her terribly—would probably never get over her passing. In his opinion, other than Crawley, she was the only other person who did not spew forth shit when she spoke. If Greta didn't have anything important to say, she wouldn't say anything at all.

They had that in common. Drake was a man of few words. Just like Crawley had been, for the most part, except maybe after half a dozen beers. Then his lips would start flapping like a Canadian flag in gale force winds.

Drake sighed. He also missed Crawley, he supposed, virtually his only connection with the human race. It didn't count when he drove into the small town of Murray Harbour for supplies. That was a necessity, and on those trips he seldom uttered two complete sentences, preferring to conduct his trade relations with a few grunts and nods.

Besides, he didn't need much. Usually, one trip to town every two months was enough to keep him going. He substituted his grocery bill with his survival skills. For a man of seventy-five, he was rugged and still pretty fit for a chain-smoker. He limited his alcohol intake to about two dozen beers a month, and most of those would usually be drained in two sittings.

He took another long drag on the rollie, enjoying the acrid taste in his lungs and throat. He stood up, donned his weathered and ripped jacket, lifted the cowboy hat from the single nail hook it hung on, and left the shack; but not before grabbing his hunting rifle. Just in case. *Time for a little hike. Exercise would be good.*

Surveying the wooded surroundings, he smiled. Nature always made him smile. Being a recluse had its perks. You could enjoy nature whenever you wanted to without worrying about what other people were doing. No one to care about in the whole world. How good was that?

He picked a well-worn path to the ocean and departed, enjoying the clear air, the chirping sounds, the thick forest surrounding him. It was just above freezing, and the afternoon sun was melting the huge snow deposit of a few days ago. Just as the calm waves of the ocean gently lapping onto shore became visible, he heard a screeching meow. It sounded like an angry cat.

Drake left the trail and walked a few feet into the bushes, toward the sound. He saw branches wriggling a few feet away and approached, rifle drawn.

He stopped when he saw it. A short-haired black cat gazed up from its kill, a large jackrabbit, its body half eaten. The cat regarded Drake cautiously with its yellow eyes, hissed, and returned to feeding on its prey, biting large chunks of rabbit flesh and devouring them quickly. Drake had never seen a cat feast so ravenously and—he hated to think of the word—rabidly.

But in spite of the visual warning, his instinct was to befriend the cat. And that was his first mistake.

"You are quite the hunter, kitty," he said, bending down and extending a hand to pat it.

"Reeeeeeeoooooooowww," was the sound it made a split second before scratching his hand and darting away.

Drake stood up, blinking in confusion. A dark rage instantly coursed through his veins. He boiled with an uncontrollable anger—an anger he knew had to be satiated immediately for it to subside.

He turned and walked purposefully toward his shack. "Fuck dinner! I think I'll go into town." Drake wasn't hungry anymore—at least not for food. He was hungry for something else—murder. He wanted to kill somebody.

And he'd be damned if he didn't get his wish.

Chapter Eleven

"If you wish," Sid Baillis said to Lori Bellafonte as they drank pints of draught beer in The Pilot House.

Lori had just told the CEO of Casinos Inc. she would never entertain a relationship with him outside the perimeters of business. And she had bravely added: "If you don't like it, or you continue hitting on me, go find yourself a new lawyer."

Now she looked him right in the eye. "Yes, I wish," she said matter-of-factly. Following Kathleen's advice, she had gone to great pains to preserve her relationship, rushing home that evening and preparing spaghetti, one of her husband's favorite foods. When he had arrived home, she had greeted him in sheer erotic lingerie, smiled seductively, curled her finger in a come-to-me-now gesture, and pulled him quickly into the apartment. By the time they had made it into the bedroom, she had already removed her negligee. While the spaghetti sauce simmered, their body temperatures boiled as they made passionate love. After the steamy session, she told Reggie about Sid's verbal advances and also announced what she had planned on doing about it.

Reggie had smiled. And in his brown eyes, she could see the rekindling of a flame that had been barely flickering. They had enjoyed a romantic candle-lit dinner and their relationship had begun to improve. Gone were Reggie's suspicious stares and questioning glances. It was time to rebuild, and her plan was working. And she wasn't prepared to ruin it for the likes of the capitalist pig sitting in front of her. Not now. Not ever. If she had once been vaguely tempted by his advances, those thoughts had all but vanished. Kathleen had been right all along. The money wasn't worth it.

She finally understood that.

Sid reached into the pocket of his black suit jacket and pulled out a small black velvet jewelry box. He pushed it across the table. "Would you accept this as a peace offering? It's a token of my appreciation for all your hard work, nothing more. I promise I'll keep our relationship strictly business."

"What is it?" Lori asked, reluctant.

"It's a gift. Open it."

She flipped open the small lid and stared down at it. At first she thought it was a necklace with a Christian cross, but then, picking it up, realized it was a gold necklace with a sword, an exact replica of the ancient sword that had purged the island of a strange and ubiquitous evil.

She wondered why Sid would buy her a gift in the first place. And why a gift that symbolized a righteous and good influence? What was he up to? He planned on opening a casino, after all. He wasn't out to save people. He wanted to make big money, knowing full well if he succeeded it would ruin the lives of many local residents. He was up to something.

"What's going on, Sid?"

"Will you accept this?"

"On one condition."

"What's that?"

"Tell me what's behind this?"

"Well, we did our research before we decided the market here could support a casino."

"I'm sure you did."

"We learned about the recent murders and mayhem on this island. And that this sword, or one like it anyway, was what saved the island's population. So, we thought what better way to welcome people into our new casino than to give them a free gift, an 18-carat gold replica of the magic sword that saved the island. They'll equate it to Casinos Inc. and support us. After all, look how many jobs we'll be creating. When it opens, Gold Rush Casino will create almost 3,000 jobs. This is going to be a tremendous boost to the local economy."

Lori had to admit he was right. It was a brilliant marketing strategy. Especially so because the company had just received approval at all government levels to build the first casino on a site just within the city limits of Charlottetown. He had planned on pushing the emotional buttons of local townsfolk to draw them in. His gift involved the use of a symbol many residents held very dear to their hearts, even if they weren't religious. His timing was perfect—a week before the ground-breaking ceremony.

"Okay," Lori said. "Thanks for this."

"Could you put it on?"

She didn't think it would hurt to humor him, especially since he had promised to cut the flirtatious advances. "Sure." She picked it up, unhooked the clasp, put it around her neck and leaned toward Sid, turning her back. "Would you mind?"

He fastened it, brushing his hand gently across her neck, and she shivered, though not because she was turned on.

"Thanks," she said, forcing a business-like smile.

"It looks beautiful on you. It compliments your black dress."

"Thanks." And after a moment's pause: "I suppose you're planning to give these away at the ground-breaking ceremony next week."

"You got it. I didn't hire you for nothing. The first five thousand people who show up for the ceremony receive free gold necklaces. We've already launched the advertising. "Now let's get down to some more business."

As Lori outlined the new tax umbrella she had devised, she couldn't help wondering what else Sid had up his sleeve involving the sword necklace. It was an unusual tact. While she couldn't put a finger on it right now—maybe that would come to her at three o'clock in the morning—she was sure about one thing.

Sid had a secret agenda.

And she knew, as sure as she was sitting in The Pilot House right now, the agenda was pure, malevolent evil.

But what was the agenda?

And what could she do about it?

Chapter Twelve

"What should we do about it?" Jacob asked Kathleen as they sat in Black Death, her trustworthy pick-up, and watched a gray Ford pick-up truck parked in front of a small general store that also served as Murray Harbour's grocery store. The old man in the truck looked intently at two customers inside the store.

"I think we should call Detective Redmond," Kathleen said. "He looks like he's stalking them or something."

"Yeah, but he hasn't done anything."

"Jacob, you know me better than that. Does he have to do something? I just have a feeling."

She was right. He nodded.

Kathleen dialed Redmond. He picked up on the first ring.

"Kathleen. I've been meaning to talk to you."

Just then, the young couple left the store. The old man stepped out of the truck, walking toward them, rifle leveled at the head of the young female.

"You need to come to Murray Harbour general store immediately," she said. "There's a murder in progress."

Gunfire exploded as Drake shot the woman once in the head. She screamed and dropped to the sidewalk. Her male companion froze in shock.

Jacob and Kathleen exited Black Death quickly.

"Hey, what are you doing?" Kathleen shouted as Drake leveled the rifle at the stunned man.

Drake turned his head. In the split second that he was distracted, the man started running down the street. Drake spun around and shot him twice in the back. The man dropped dead with a loud groan.

Drake popped another round in the side chamber, turned and walked toward Kathleen and Jacob, his eyes glazed and empty.

They were crouched behind Black Death. "Get in," Jacob shouted.

Kathleen slid in and stayed down. She had known with finality when they had rolled to a stop outside the store and saw the old man peering in the window at the customers that someone was going to die. And that there wasn't a damn thing she could do about it.

Jacob climbed in the driver seat. The engine was still running. Kathleen sprawled out along the back seat.

Drake, a twisted look of unfathomable rage contorting his features, steadied the firearm at Jacob's head.

Jacob revved the motor. He had two choices: drive toward his attacker and mow him down, or back up while being fired at. And he only had a split second to make up his mind. He popped it into drive and ploughed forward.

A bullet crashed through the windshield as Black Death smashed into Drake. Drake's body crunched off the hood, smashed the windshield, and rolled off into the snow with a thud.

Detective Redmond screeched to a stop, exited his vehicle, and started shouting.

Jacob stopped the truck.

He and Kathleen glanced behind them through the shattered glass. The bullet had narrowly missed Jacob's head and broken the front and rear windshields. Drake stood up, staggering around on broken limbs, and managed to pick up the rifle. A large gash above his eye spurted blood as he advanced.

"Shit, he's going to shoot us again," Kathleen said. "Get the hell out of here."

Jacob slammed the vehicle into drive. He was about to floor it but heard the crack of a gunshot.

Drake turned around to face a shouting Redmond. He leveled the gun at the detective but Redmond shot him in the head. Drake dropped to the snow, a howling cry escaping his lips. His body twitched for a few seconds and became limp.

Kathleen and Jacob stepped out of the truck. Sirens wailed in the distance. The elderly female shopkeeper stood outside the store, staring down at the body of the first female victim. A few cars stopped on Main Street and people gawked at the carnage.

"Don't go near the body," Redmond said as he approached them. "Are you okay?"

Kathleen and Jacob were white-faced. Kathleen nodded.

"I didn't have a choice," Jacob said, pointing to the shattered windshield. "He was trying to kill us."

"I can see that. Don't worry. You won't be implicated in this. I saw him shoot at you."

Soon the area was abuzz with police, an ambulance, and forensics experts. The scene was taped off as investigators did their work and ambulance crews removed the corpses.

Police Constable Reggie Snyden and Detective Russ Willard arrived at the scene. Redmond gave them a brief explanation of events and put Willard in charge.

Kathleen and Jacob sat in Black Death with the motor running, waiting for further instructions from Redmond.

"Can you handle this?" Redmond asked Willard.

"Sure, boss," the young detective said.

"I want you to be very careful with the body of the shooter," Redmond said.

Willard nodded.

"Have you found the cat?" Redmond asked.

"Not yet. But we will," Willard said. "You think the shooter's infected?"

"I don't know. But I'm sure as hell not taking any chances."

"I'm going to leave you with this and take Jacob and Kathleen home." Investigators would be combing over Black Death for evidence before the vehicle would be released back into Kathleen's hands.

Redmond eyeballed the scene for clues one last time.

Snyden stood at Black Death, talking to Kathleen, who sat in the driver seat, Jacob beside her. "I just wanted to apologize for my sarcastic comments the other day," Snyden said. "Willard and Redmond filled me in on your abilities and, while I don't really believe in psychic stuff, they say you provided critical information on previous investigations. I'm sorry about that."

"No problem," Kathleen said, suspecting the cop had another agenda.

"I know something else," he said.

"Oh, what's that?"

"I know you saw my wife, Lori."

Kathleen's face reddened. Lori said she wouldn't tell Snyden anything, but had obviously changed her mind. "Oh."

"Don't worry," Snyden said. "I'm not mad or anything. Since her visit with you, our relationship couldn't be better. I don't know what you discussed, but it sure as hell worked. I wanted to thank you."

"No problem. It felt good to be on the other side of carnage for a change. "I'm glad to hear it helped."

"It did," Snyden said. "Thanks again."

Willard waved him over.

"I've got to go," he said. He took a few steps and stopped. "Just curious. Did you get any feeling on this crazy shit that just happened here?"

Kathleen nodded. Snyden raised an eyebrow, turned, and walked away.

A few minutes later, Kathleen and Jacob sat in Redmond's unmarked Crown Vic as he drove them home. Kathleen sat in front, Jacob in back.

After an uncomfortable silence, Redmond said: "Kathleen, I have to say, death seems to follow you. What's with that, anyway?"

"If I knew, you'd be the first to know." She wasn't sure that was true, but thought it sounded good. She didn't have a better answer right now. "At least I got a feeling and called you right away—even though it was a little late."

"Better late than never," Redmond said, scratching his stubble and goatee. It made the sound of sandpaper on wood. "I'd like to ask you something."

"Go ahead."

"I'd like to use you occasionally. I think, with your psychic powers, it would be good to have you during investigations.

That way, we might be able to prevent some of this before it happens. What do you think?"

"I wouldn't be adverse—especially if it means saving lives."

"Are you up for it? Mentally, I mean?"

Kathleen knew her anxiety attacks in the past had become public knowledge. Certainly Redmond was well aware of them. He had driven her to the hospital a few times when the attacks had led to complete catatonia. She knew she had been feeling a little anxious lately, but the calm lake metaphor was still helping. And she was medication-free. Her head felt a lot clearer. "I think I am."

"Okay, that settles it then. I'll let you know when I need you. And I'll try and give you as much notice as possible. The department will pay you. I have a special fund for the resources of special people."

"Okay." Kathleen didn't care how much she was being paid. It didn't matter. What did matter was getting to the bottom of the Rage Virus, if that's what they were dealing with, before it decimated the entire island population.

"What about me?" Jacob asked. "Don't you have a fund for a talented guy like me?"

Redmond chuckled. "I'm sorry, buddy. It ain't gonna happen."

"Have you found out anything more about Crawley?" Kathleen said.

"I talked to his niece and daughter the other day. They say there was no reason to suspect he would do anything like this. They knew he was having a hard time with the death of his wife. But not hard enough to kill himself."

"And the necklace?"

"That's a bit of a mystery. We know it was purchased through Casinos Inc. under a numbered company, and is being sold in a few jewelry stores—one here, another in Halifax. Lori Bellafonte—I believe you know her—said Casinos Inc. plans on distributing them free to the people who attend the ground-breaking ceremony in a week. There's a Sid Baillis, whom Lori is suspicious of, who's in charge of this casino venture."

"What do you think of Baillis?"

"I don't know. Haven't talked to him yet. That's your first assignment. I want your read on him. He does make me wonder, especially since Lori is suspicious. She's a damn good lawyer with a sharp instinct for people."

"What about the necklace? Why would he pick that sword?"

"I don't know. Maybe he thinks the townsfolk will appreciate the positive symbol, and it'll benefit his planned casino. If he has something else in mind, I have no idea what it is."

"And the Rage Virus? Do you think it's somehow connected to Baillis?"

"That's a shot in the dark ... no pun intended. I have no idea. I have absolutely no evidence to suggest that. That's where you come in."

"Have you found the cat yet?"

"No, but we will. Is your cat inside?"

"Yeah," Kathleen said. "Ever since Crawley said he was scratched by a cat, I haven't let her out. I don't want her getting mixed up with the fugitive feline."

Jacob and Redmond chuckled in spite of themselves.

"That cat is a short-haired black cat. Spike has long hair. Am I right?"

"You are," she said. "But I don't want to take any chances."

"Good idea."

There was another long moment of silence before Jacob broke it: "You think Drake was infected?"

"Yes, I do. This is totally out of character for him. There are a few cops heading over to his shack right now to search for the cat. We found a scratch on Drake's hand. Also, Crawley was pretty much the only friend he had. Crawley might have been scratched at Drake's shack."

They digested the news.

Not good, Kathleen thought. First, they had an infected feline running around scratching people who became infected and either killed others or themselves. Where in the hell did this virus come from? Secondly, and it might be nothing, there was a businessman intent on wooing casino supporters by giving them free gold necklaces, with the very same sword that had saved the island a few months ago. What was with that anyway? How come Crawley had one of these necklaces? Did he know something?

And what about her weird experience the other night with Mark? It wasn't really Mark in the flesh; it was Mark in Jacob's body. They had made love. But Jacob had no recollection of the event. In Kathleen's eyes, it wasn't Jacob at all, didn't even remotely resemble him. The spirit world and the strange events around town lately *were* actually beginning to wreak havoc on her psyche. She wondered if she should call her doctor and request a prescription of anti-anxiety pills to carry her over the crest of this tsunami wave of carnage.

She pushed the thought from her mind and returned her thoughts to Jacob. After the intimate experience at her house, there had been an uncomfortable silence between them that had lasted for a few days before she had finally broken down and picked up the phone, asking for his company. Again. But what had started off as a pleasant drive to Murray Harbour had ended in disaster and had almost gotten them killed.

That was it, she decided. It was time to bring everything out in the open. Neither of them had been willing to talk about their lovemaking sessions. But, if their friendship meant anything, now was the time to clear the air. With all the shit going on around them, Kathleen wasn't prepared to complicate her life any further. Not now. Not anymore.

Redmond pulled up to Kathleen's house, where Jacob had parked his SUV. "I'll let you know when I need you." Redmond looked at them with concern. "Have a good night. Be careful."

They stood outside, watching his Crown Vic pull away. Jacob had his hands in his pockets, refusing eye contact. He swept his gaze around the street as if awaiting someone's arrival. "I should go. It's getting late."

"Jacob." Kathleen grabbed his arm. "Could you come inside? There's something I need to talk to you about."

Jacob paused for a moment and looked at the sidewalk. Then he slowly looked up, nodded and they walked toward her house. Kathleen went in while Jacob stood outside, smoking a cigar. He said his nerves were a little rattled and he needed a smoke to calm down. She didn't argue.

"Join me on the couch when you're done."

Chapter Thirteen

They sat side-by-side on Kathleen's couch, sipping tea from large blue mugs. Spike watched wearily, crouched underneath the television stand.

"I think you know what this is about," Kathleen said, taking a sip and setting her mug on the coffee table.

Jacob nodded.

"There are some forces at work here which, at least for the time being, are beyond our control. And I think we need to get it out in the open."

He nodded again.

"Those intimate times we had together ... uh, that wasn't really us. Or, at least it wasn't one of us. You know that, don't you?"

"Yeah, if it weren't for the telltale physical signs that something happened and some odd fleeting images, I never would have thought it was real."

"I know what you mean. Some part of me wanted to believe that Mark was alive again. But I think we both know that's not the case."

"I suppose it depends on your definition of alive," Jacob said philosophically. "When you were with Mark, I literally wasn't there. He was in my body, in my mind. I completely blanked out during the whole thing."

"Same for me when you were with Angela. But I don't want this to come between us. That's what's been happening."

"I know. It's just ... I like and respect you so much as a friend I felt I ... somehow breached that."

"You didn't breach anything. It was Mark. And I didn't breach anything. It was Angela. Why should we hold ourselves accountable for their actions?"

"You're right. But you have to admit, this is getting pretty fucked up."

"It is," Kathleen said. "I guess we have to figure out what we can do about it."

"I guess so."

"Tell me—and I don't mean to pry—how are you doing? I mean, how are you coping with Angela's death?"

"I'm starting to feel better. But probably still a long way from where I need to be." Jacob didn't want to mention the black cloud of depression that had been exponentially growing until the recent appearance of Angela. He was talking to a psychic, after all. She probably already knew. "What about you?"

"Same. And like you, things started to get a lot better when Mark showed up the other day." There was a pause, and then she added: "Do you know, sometimes Angela speaks to me. Like Liz a few months back, I can hear her talking inside my head."

"That's weird." But he knew it wasn't weird. Not for Kathleen, anyway. "What does she say to you?"

"Oh, I don't know. Nothing scary. Mostly reassuring stuff. You know how Angela was."

"An angel," Jacob said, his eyes going far away. "What should we do?"

"Well, if you think about it, the reason they're back is for us. They're here for our happiness. I also think they want us to know the place they're in isn't bad. It obviously allows them to check up on us, even rekindle the romances. But I don't think I can carry on like this. You?"

"Well, they're borrowing our bodies and minds, and in a way preventing us from moving on. I'm sure they don't realize it, but ultimately I agree with you. In the long term, I don't think it's helping us. Still. Back to the question: What do we do?"

"I've been thinking of a séance. If we can contact them, explain how dear they are to us, but gently tell them we don't want them possessing us, maybe they'll go away."

Jacob thought about the depth of his love for Angela, and in that moment wasn't sure anything could replace it. "Do you really want that?"

Kathleen thought about it. "I wouldn't mind seeing the ghost of Mark occasionally, but I don't really want him attaching his spirit to you to do it. Let's face it—it's interfering with our friendship." *And possibly a little more*, Kathleen thought, but didn't want to go there. At least not right this minute.

He thought about it. "I guess you're right. I wouldn't mind seeing the ghost of Angela, at least to know she's safe and happy. But I would rather she didn't possess you to accomplish that. When do you want to do it?"

"I'll get a feeling when the time is right. I'm going to try calling Angela out on my own a few times, make some suggestions. If I can feel her presence, I'll know it's time. I'll let you know."

"That would be great." Jacob breathed a sigh of relief. He had felt conflicted for the last week or so about the strange intimacies he had shared with his best friend, and he felt a lot better now that everything was out in the open. And they had a plan.

They finished their tea, talking for a while longer.

"I better go," Jacob said finally. "I appreciate this, Kathleen. You always seem to know what to do."

"Thanks." Kathleen felt quite the opposite, but wasn't going to argue. They hugged—a long, tight embrace—and Jacob left.

She felt better, at least about her best friend.

Chapter Fourteen

The diminutive bald man in the white lab coat felt better. He had finally discovered a formula that was working. At least, he thought so. He pulled the sword necklace out of the liquid carefully with gloved hands and tweezers. He wore an oxygen mask attached to a small cylindrical tank. He wasn't going to take any chances. Not with this stuff. He set the necklace on a napkin on a table cluttered with chemistry equipment and stared at it for a moment. Under the bright laboratory lights, he could almost see the liquid drying.

A cage rattled and a monkey squealed.

He approached a wooden box beside the monkey cage, pulled out two bananas, and tossed them beside the cage. The monkey screeched, examined the bananas that were out of reach and eyed his captor curiously.

"It's almost time," the man said. "You know the drill."

He picked up the necklace and returned to the cage. The liquid was dry. He held the necklace up and the monkey immediately ran to the edge of the cage, offering his back so the man could fasten it around his neck.

He had been Pavlovian-conditioned for the response. Once the necklace was around his neck, he would be fed.

The man fastened the necklace and the monkey reared back, screeching. *Good,* the man thought.

He picked up the bananas and handed them through the cage to the monkey, who quickly grabbed them, peeled one and began taking large bites, occasionally glancing at the man curiously.

"Good boy," the man said and left.

Dressed in his white lab coat and wearing the same full-face oxygen mask, he returned twenty-four hours later and smiled at the result of his experiment.

The monkey was banging on the metal bars, twisting, turning and screeching. He bared his teeth and uttered a threatening growl.

He was out of his mind with rage.

The man checked the video camera to make sure it was still on and left. He was convinced he didn't need to go over the data. It had taken him months to get it right. But he would, anyway. Why not? He was being paid big money for his little experiments.

The man left the lab, sealed the door shut, and walked down a corridor into a small office. He removed his mask and set it on a coat hanger, then sat down at a desk piled high with papers and picked up his cell phone.

On the second ring, from his luxurious Charlottetown third-floor office, Sid Baillis picked up one of two cell phones he had in his suit pocket. He recognized the number and got right to the point. "Tell me you've got something that works, Rex."

"Yes, we do," Rex Robertson said. "It works better than I could've imagined."

"Have you gone over the video?"

"Not yet, but I will. I'm sure you won't be disappointed."

"Go over the video," Sid said, annoyed that Rex might have called prematurely. "And if you find anything out of the ordinary, call me immediately."

"Don't worry," Rex said. "I'm sure you'll be hap ..."

Baillis saw the red button on the phone system beep. That meant something urgent. "I have to go," he said, killing the call and stuffing the pay-as-you-go disposable phone back into his suit jacket.

He pressed the red button and the intercom came to life. "Mr. Baillis, sir," said Veronica Hills, his attractive, middle-aged secretary in her usual seductive voice. "There's a Detective Redmond and a Kathleen here to see you. They don't have an appointment. What should I tell them?"

Sid thought about it for a minute. Detective Redmond and Kathleen? His men had done a little research on the pair. He hoped they weren't planning on bringing him any trouble. If they were, he already had plan B in place to deal with them. And it didn't involve a lot of verbal diarrhea either. If he put them off, that would arouse suspicion. And so far, the plan was going letter-perfect. He made a snap decision.

"Did they say what they wanted?"

"Something about the upcoming ground-breaking ceremony for the casino."

Hell, it was probably just traffic control cop shit. "See them in."

The door opened and Redmond and Kathleen entered.

"I don't believe we've met," Baillis said, shaking hands. His muscle-bound six-foot-four frame dwarfed the visitors. "I'm Sid Baillis, CEO of Casinos Inc."

"Blaine Redmond and Kathleen Freeborne," Redmond said.

He offered them a seat and a drink. They took the seat, declined the drink. Although it was certainly past noon in many countries, it was only 10:46 am in Charlottetown. A little early to start drinking—at least for Redmond and Kathleen.

"What can I do for you?" His black hair was pulled back in a ponytail, his olive-toned skin and chiseled features a picture of toughness and health. His white teeth were perfectly aligned. His brown eyes darted from Kathleen to Redmond.

He looks like he's hiding something, Kathleen thought. *But what?*

"I just thought I'd drop in to see if PEI's finest can offer you any additional help for the big ground-breaking ceremony coming up next Saturday," Redmond said, while Kathleen sat quietly, allowing her sixth sense do the work.

"I talked to your chief," Baillis said. "Whiting, I think it is?"

"That's him," Redmond said. He was walking a political tightrope. Whiting had told him not to bother Baillis, the man who would soon pull the small city from its economic woes. Unemployment was at an all-time high. And, with the promise of 3,000 new jobs, Baillis had become a local hero. The city mayor had instructed Whiting to be nice to Baillis, and Whiting had made that abundantly clear to the force.

Baillis cleared his throat. "Whiting has everything covered as far as traffic goes. He's going to block off part of University Avenue and Allen Street."

"I wasn't aware," Redmond lied. "Sometimes one department doesn't communicate with the other. You know how that goes."

Baillis nodded.

"What about police presence? Are you covered there?"

Baillis looked pensive. "I think Whiting has ten men on it."

"I think I'll add another five, just to be sure," Redmond said. "I can pull some of my detectives in for you if you like."

Baillis didn't see the point in arguing about police presence. "Whatever you think is best."

They talked briefly about the benefits the new casino would bring to Charlottetown and the island. Baillis said he was looking forward to helping the small province. Kathleen sat quietly the entire time, nodding at the right times, contributing the odd yes when she thought it was appropriate.

Baillis's brown eyes darkened, if only for a split second, and he said to Kathleen: "I hear you're a local hero ... with your psychic abilities?"

The question took Kathleen by surprise and her face reddened. "So they tell me."

"Tell me," he said, "do you have visions?"

"Sometimes." She didn't know where he was going with this, but didn't like the vibe she got as soon as she walked in the door. It wasn't anything pervasive, but it was there, lingering like a thick gray cloud does before booming with thunder and unleashing a deadly battery of hailstones onto unsuspecting victims.

"Can you see anything in my future?" he asked.

There was a brief pause while Kathleen thought. "These psychic feelings, or visions, don't always manifest themselves on demand." She would answer his questions only. She didn't want to elaborate. *Keep it simple stupid.*

"That means you can't see anything in my future right now. No vibe, or whatever, one way or the other?"

"Nothing." Kathleen shook her head for emphasis.

Redmond didn't like where this was going. He was supposed to be the one steering the conversation, but things had turned. He noticed a sword necklace glittering on Baillis's neck. "Interesting marketing gimmick," he said, pointing to it. "Was that your idea?"

Baillis smiled a fake smile and eyed the detective curiously. "As a matter of fact, it was. Good omen, I believe."

There was an uncomfortable silence before Redmond decided one more tactic was necessary to try to find a chink in the armor. He had no doubt it was there. He cast his eyes to the magnificent view of historic downtown, Charlottetown harbor in the background. Then he slowly fixed his gaze on Baillis while Kathleen squirmed in the black leather chair. "Too bad Jonathon Crawley didn't have one around his neck before he died."

The CEO's expression went blank. "I'm sorry, detective, I don't follow you."

"A local resident recently blew his brains out with a shotgun." Redmond pointed again to the necklace. "We found one of those in his bedroom dresser drawer."

Baillis had run out of patience. His brow furrowed as he stared at the detective. "I'm not sure where you're going with this, or how this possibly concerns me, but I don't like it."

Enough was enough. Redmond certainly didn't want a tongue-lashing from Stan Whiting. And he knew if he kept up this questioning, one would certainly be forthcoming. He'd probably gone too far already. It was time to kiss some ass. "I'm sorry, sir. It was just an off-handed comment. I didn't mean to offend you."

But he could see he had offended Baillis. Controlled anger seethed below the calm exterior. They were ushered out the door in a tone and demeanor that fell short of friendly.

Baillis slowly shook his head as he stood at the expansive window, watching them get in the black car and drive away.

He had two calls to make. He fished a cell phone from his pocket. A deep voice answered on the first ring. "Kathleen Freeborne and Detective Redmond," Baillis said.

"What about them?" the killer asked.

"Keep an eye on them."

"Is that all?"

"Until you hear otherwise." He hung up the phone and reached for the other one.

He dialed a number and the soft-spoken chemist answered on the third ring. "Do you have the formula?"

"I'm ninety-nine percent sure we do, Sid," Rex said.

Baillis bristled. "I told you never to call me by name. Did you leave your fucking brain at home today? And I don't want to hear ninety-nine percent. Call me when you're one hundred percent. I'm not leaving anything to chance. You hear me?"

"Yes, sir," Rex said in an agitated tone.

Sid hung up.

Chapter Fifteen

"I wouldn't be too hung up on it, honey," Reddie Snyden said to Lori. They sat on a brown leather couch in their upscale condo a few short blocks from Sid's prestigious office.

Snyden knew his wife wasn't an idiot. Truth be told, she was probably his intellectual superior, although he wouldn't admit it. If she suspected something was wrong, it probably was. She had been questioned by Detective Redmond, who said he planned on paying Baillis a visit.

"I don't think I'm hung up on anything, Reg. I just smell a rat, that's all."

He nodded. He hated admitting when she was right. He also knew it was one of the issues he would have to overcome if he planned on staying with Lori. After all, wasn't it better that she suspect Baillis of something devious than have an affair with him?

"What do you want me to do about it? Redmond's on it, and he's the best detective we got."

"I know," Lori said resignedly. "I thought Kathleen was the one with the visions and extrasensory perception, but my gut's telling me something's wrong here."

Snyden wasn't going to touch the comment about Kathleen. While he didn't believe in all that psychic mumbo jumbo, Kathleen had certainly said something that had changed his and Lori's relationship for the better. He was more deeply in love with his wife now than he had ever been. Something *had* happened during her little visit with the town psychic.

He bit his tongue and stared at the small cut on his index finger—the worst place on the hand to get a cut. So small, yet it stung like hell. He examined it more closely while his wife went into the kitchen for another bottle of wine. His finger was now red and swollen. His mind raced. *Shit. Where did I get that again?* Then the memory came to him in a flash and he shuddered as a wave of panic swept over him. After Black Death had been hauled into one of the bays at the station, he had gone to see forensics technician Stan Neiderman. He wanted to pick his brain and impress his partner, Detective Russ Willard. He had absently run his hand across the hood of the truck while talking to Stan, and the man had said, "Hold up there, my friend. That could be contaminated blood on that hood."

Snyden had jerked his hand away, examined it, but didn't notice anything. A few minutes later, back in the station, he noticed the small cut. There must have been a metal burr sticking out of the hood that had pierced his finger. Or he could have gotten it somewhere else. He wasn't sure.

He had spent the day in search of the infected feline, and the whole incident had slipped his mind. He had been thinking of more carnal things, such as the sexual experimentation he and his wife had recently engaged in that had aroused him so much he couldn't get the episodes out of his mind—and couldn't wait to get home to resume these heated and satisfying extra-curricular activities.

So the little cut had completely left his mind. Until now.

Lori returned, smiling. She had opened a bottle of red wine and undone the buttons on her satin white blouse just enough to expose a healthy amount of cleavage.

Snyden felt an inexplicable aggression take hold. He had briefed her on the Rage Virus, or the suspicion of the virus. He had warned her to take it deadly serious and avoid anyone acting weird. And he meant it.

Lori stopped in the middle of the living room, noticing her husband's reddened face and odd expression of despair. "Honey, what's wrong?"

"Don't come near me," he demanded.

"What?"

"STAY THE FUCK AWAY FROM ME!"

She took a few steps back, dropping the open wine bottle on the new beige shag carpet, its contents spilling out and staining the rug red. She bent down to pick it up but stopped abruptly, staring at the ugly transformation taking place in her soul mate.

Snyden could feel his temperature rising, the hot anger suffusing his being, his face flushing with its evil force. He knew he couldn't control it. He narrowed his eyes and glared at the beautiful woman standing in front of him. There was only one thing he wanted to do to her right now.

He wanted to murder her in a brutal fashion. With what remained of his rational self, he said one more thing to his beloved wife before the rage seized him completely and rendered his mind a bastion for evil intentions: "GET THE FUCK OUT OF HERE NOW!"

Reggie Snyden was no longer himself. He had become an angry and powerful monster with a singular purpose—to kill.

Lori didn't need a kick in the ass at that point. She quickly grabbed her jacket and ran out of the condo, down the hall, wondering grimly how much longer she had to live.

She glanced back as she ran. Snyden was right behind her, waving his gun, his eyes wild. He was growling like a possessed madman who had erroneously been released from an insane asylum.

She quickly ran passed the elevator and headed for the stairwell. She jerked the door open just as a bullet whistled past her head and ripped into the drywall with a crunching sound.

He was gaining on her.

She could hear him growling as she darted down the stairs, the concrete walls amplifying the sound and echoing it eerily throughout the narrow stairwell. She was panting by the time she reached the main floor. *Shit. This story isn't going to have a happy ending.*

She ran out onto Kent Street, waving her hands, and then a thought entered her mind. She had her cell phone in her jacket pocket. She was sure of it. She heard the crack of gunfire behind her as she turned right and darted between two old brick apartment buildings. A black cat hissed, yowled, and scurried across her path. She felt in her pocket.

It was there.

She ran into the back alley, accidentally kicking over a metal garbage can. It clanged and rolled down the alley, debris spilling out. The night was dark, chilly, and windy. She spotted a small white fence, quickly climbed over it, and crouched down.

She had put a little distance between her and Snyden. But she could still hear the growling, faint at first, but growing louder. Terrified, she ran across the residential backyard and ducked into a metal storage shed. She pulled out the phone and speed-dialed Detective Redmond. He had asked her to put his number on speed dial after their last meeting. She was grateful she had followed his instructions.

He picked up on the first ring. "Reggie's been infected. He's trying to kill me." She could hardly control the rising panic in her voice.

"Where are you?" Redmond asked. He didn't know it at the time, but he was only a few short blocks away, doing unauthorized surveillance outside the office of Sid Baillis. He had been sitting in his car, peering up at the lit office with a pair of binoculars, when she called.

"I'm in the alley, just down from my place." She took a few deep breaths. "Kent and Weymouth Street."

"And Reggie?"

"He's coming after me."

"I'll be right there. Don't hang up." He clicked the speaker on, threw the smartphone on the passenger seat, and fired up the Crown Vic.

Less than a minute later, he pulled down the alley. The headlights illuminated the back of Snyden, a white t-shirt, jeans, bare feet, approaching a white fence, gun drawn.

He pulled alongside, stopped the car, jumped out and crouched behind it, leveling his gun at the enraged monster. "PUT THAT GUN DOWN, SNYDEN."

Snyden spun around, and with empty and unfocused eyes, fired. The bullet ripped into the front fender of the vehicle as Redmond ducked. Two more shots—crack, crack—whizzed by the detective's head.

Snyden had stopped growling. He calmly walked toward the vehicle with the intention of walking around it and emptying the chamber into the crouched detective's head.

Redmond only had a split second to react. He popped his head out and shot Snyden in the leg.

Snyden reached for his leg, stumbled, and fell face-first. As he started to get up, Redmond raced out from behind the car, raised his police baton, and struck Snyden hard in the back of the head. Snyden fell face-first again into the slush, his body spasmodically twitching before going limp.

Redmond heard the sobs before recognizing her. Lori, her face wet with tears, peered over the white fence, saw her lifeless husband and let out a heart-wrenching scream, followed by more loud and wracking sobs.

"Don't go near that body," Redmond ordered. "He's not your husband anymore. He's a killer."

Chapter Sixteen

The killer sat in his car near the house, eyeing the bay window. It was late evening and he was watching Kathleen and Jacob with a pair of binoculars. An ex-Navy SEAL turned rogue hitman, Bain Derksen wondered if he should just get it over with and get the fuck out of here. He didn't like authority at the best of times, and if wasn't for the large sums of money Baillis was paying him, he would have told the control freak to fuck off and die a long time ago. Maybe he would tell him to fuck off and even help him with the latter part.

He lit another smoke, took a long drag and pulled his metal whiskey flask from the glove compartment. He took a swig, enjoying the strong taste as it washed down his throat, closed it, and popped it back in its place. Bain only had two vices—well, three, if you counted his penchant for visiting prostitutes. Which he didn't count. He figured getting his rocks off was a necessity, not a vice. Everyone, unless they're nearly dead, drugged, depressed, physically ill, has to have biological urges satisfied. That's the way Bain saw it. So he viewed his visits with prostitutes three times a week as a hobby and a biological necessity more than anything.

Yeah, that's it, a hobby. A hobby that occasionally resulted in one or more hookers getting a few hard punches to the face. Or, as in at least two instances, the shit kicked out of them and multiple stab wounds.

But Bain didn't have a conscience about that. If they wanted to get mouthy with him, they deserved what they got. They had it coming. Period. A month or so ago, after he had beaten one twenty-five-year-old hooker to a pulp and then stabbed her repeatedly, he suddenly developed an appetite. So he had ordered a pizza, sat in an easy chair watching *Wheel of Fortune*, mimicking the contestant's responses. He was trying to beat them to the answers, but on that particular evening in Halifax, he wasn't quite fast enough.

Not that the dead and bleeding Lola on the bed beside him was a distraction, though. No. It had nothing to do with that. He hardly glanced at her as he watched the game show, munching on his pepperoni pizza. When he did, a slow smile brightened his face. She had gotten what she deserved. No. It wasn't Lola at all. He was just a little tired that day. That was all.

And, if he had to be completely honest with himself, perhaps a little drunk also.

But he wanted to get this business over with as soon as possible. He had heard the police were getting closer and he didn't want to be around when they got too close for comfort.

When he finished with the PEI assignment, he planned on leaving the country for good. He had a connection down in Ecuador and knew the money he had saved, plus what he would receive from Baillis, would be more than enough to retire there. His cellmate Rudy had done it on a hell of a lot less. And, according to Rudy, the booze, hookers and accommodation were cheap. Hell, he could retire there on $700 a month if he really wanted to. But he had become accustomed to the good life, and wanted to be able to spend a little more than that. Bain was thinking along the lines of maybe $5,000 a month. On that money, he could live like a king—not King Shit of Turd Mountain either.

It would only be him, after all. Bain knew from his only long-term relationship, a three-year marriage with Lenora, that he wasn't cut out for that kind of commitment. His assignments in Iraq and Afghanistan had probably contributed to that, but he didn't care anymore. Initially after returning from covert killing operations, he had been traumatized by the events. Post-Traumatic Stress Disorder, his shrink had called it. He had become miserable, haunted by nightmares of murder, and it eventually led to physical and psychological abuse of Lenora. After returning from her third visit to the hospital, bandaged and bruised, she had packed up their seven-year-old son, Tyler, and left him.

She didn't know it, but the timing couldn't have been better. Bain had been planning to kill her.

The nightmares of murder and bloodshed had started to become more than that. They became dreams that he enjoyed—that feeling of being in complete control of another person's life. After a while, without that control, he had felt a vacuum in his life. A vacuum that he knew could only be filled by the thrill of the kill. So five years ago, when he met Sid Baillis in a Toronto night club, he had decided to become a hitman, give up the dumpy one-bedroom apartment he had been renting, and begin a new career, one that would involve a more transient lifestyle that would allow him to pursue his passion.

But life on the road had been taking its toll. He longed to set down roots in a country far away from the invasive eyes of the police. After all, he wasn't young anymore. He was 58, but sure didn't look it. He was six-foot-five, with a hundred and eighty-five pound muscular frame, a shaved head, a small goatee and sharp, beady brown eyes. His appearance would change as required. He knew the police were looking for a two-hundred pound man with long, wavy brown hair, glasses, and a full beard. Bain looked nothing like that now.

He had notched fifty-six kills on his belt. Twenty-five of them on SEAL operations and the other twenty-six were contract killings ordered by Baillis. When someone got in the way of a project, or even if Baillis thought they would get in the way, it was off with their head.

Figuratively, of course.

Bain generally preferred clean, quick, execution-style killings that involved his nine millimeter semi-automatic Glock. Only occasionally, and he'd have to really be in the mood for it, he didn't mind a little slash and dash with the sharp blade of his military-issue combat knife.

He scratched his goatee, adjusted his baseball cap, and pulled out the flask; a few more nips and then call it a night. He wasn't getting much here anyway. He would've liked to finish them both off. Regrettably, that would have to wait a little longer. But not too much longer, he hoped, as he felt the alcohol slowly begin to dull his senses. He wanted to get the hell off this shitty island with the shitty weather.

Chapter Seventeen

"What the hell are you doing with those?" Kathleen asked, staring at the pistols Jacob had placed on the coffee table.

She stared at two semi-automatic .45 Caliber M 1911 pistols, standard US military-issue from 1911 to 1985.

"You don't think it's about time we started arming ourselves?"

Redmond had brought them up to speed. Authorities were inches away from declaring an epidemic. The only thing stopping them was the upcoming ground-breaking ceremony. The almighty dollar had been put ahead of public health and safety.

In spite of her dislike for firearms, Kathleen had to admit he had a point. "Where did you get these?"

"Let's just say a little bird gave them to me." Actually, he had bought them off the internet. It was easy to acquire unlicensed firearms in this day and age, a grim testament to what the world was coming to.

"Are they loaded?"

"Oh yeah."

"You want me to walk around with a gun?"

"I don't think it's a bad idea. Particularly in light of all the shit happening. You said you're worried about what Sid Baillis is up to."

Kathleen *was* worried. Last night she'd had a vision of an enraged monster pursuing a terrified woman down an alley, firing a gun. When she had called Redmond, he had told her about Snyden's attack on Lori. The details were eerily similar to her vision. She had started hyperventilating on her couch, almost to the point of losing consciousness. When her head finally cleared, she called her doctor, arranged for a prescription of anti-anxiety meds, left the house to retrieve them, then returned and fell into a troubled and fitful sleep.

The edge was back, all right. And it was snapping loudly inside her head, wanting to come out to play.

Kathleen nodded and Jacob gave her a quick lesson in firearms handling. A few minutes later, she thought she could handle the weapon. Even though she had never fired a gun in her life and never believed she would ever have the need to. But now things were different. Now she felt sure the gun she gripped would one day save her life.

The wind howled and brushed some tree branches against the bay window. Kathleen absently approached the window, casting her eyes down the street. She had noticed a black car there earlier and frowned as she realized it was still there. She could see the small orange dot of a cigarette, fading and then brightening in the darkness.

A chill crept up her spine. "I don't like the looks of that car."

"What car?"

"That black car over there. I noticed it earlier."

"Why didn't you say something?"

"I didn't want you to think I'm being paranoid."

"Kathleen, I've known you long enough to trust your instincts."

"Yeah, but the panic attacks. I'm told that's all paranoid stuff."

"How long has it been since you've had a panic attack?"

"I don't know. Two, three months."

"I'd say you're doing pretty well."

"I don't know about that, Jacob. I filled a prescription today, took some pills."

"We've been through some scary shit together lately. When was the last time I intentionally mowed someone down with Black Death?"

Kathleen knew it was a rhetorical question. And she knew if he hadn't done it, they might not be having this conversation. They might both be dead.

"You saved my life, Jacob. Thanks for that, by the way."

There was a long pause. "Not a problem."

She continued staring out the window, worry wrinkling her brow. "I think we should call Redmond."

"It's your call." Jacob knew better than to second-guess her. "Ah, no pun intended."

They laughed nervously.

She called the detective and explained her fears about the black car. Redmond said he was working in Charlottetown, a thirty-minute drive from Montague. He offered to leave his post or, if she wanted more immediate assistance, to call Detective Russ Willard.

"Thirty minutes is okay," she said. Kathleen liked Willard but had a much better rapport with Redmond. They had been through a lot together, even become co-workers. She hung up as Jacob's expression brightened marginally.

"Look," he said. "The car's leaving."

Kathleen breathed a sigh of relief. But she wasn't sure they were out of immediate danger.

They sat on the couch in silence.

Spike slithered into the living room. Her yellow eyes were wild, as if she too suspected some imminent danger. "Come here, Spike," Kathleen said. The cat meowed and quickly darted into the kitchen, leaping onto the counter and arching her back.

It happened so fast, Kathleen barely had time to think. The back door suddenly crashed open and a man wearing a balaclava burst into the kitchen with a gun. Spike hissed and leaped onto the intruder's head, meowing angrily and digging her claws in deep. The man staggered, an incomprehensible pain-filled threat leaving his lips as he raised his right hand and struggled to dislodge his unexpected attacker.

"What the fuck," Jacob shouted.

Kathleen didn't wait around to see what happened next. She tucked the gun in her pocket and turned to Jacob. "Let's go ... now!"

He grabbed a gun and they raced from the house. As they climbed into the SUV, Kathleen glanced back and heard the crack of gunfire. The intruder had dislodged Spike and was standing at the door, firing. Two bullets crunched into the fender as they sped away.

Spike had saved their lives. At least for the time being.

"Where are you going?" she asked as Jacob careened around a corner. The SUV lost traction for a second, sliding out briefly before he regained control.

"The highway. Let's get the fuck out of town."

Kathleen didn't have time to decide if it was a good idea. Her hands were trembling so she stuffed them in her pockets, where the cell phone was supposed to be. She felt both pockets. It wasn't there. She felt the panic rising in her throat as the realization hit her. "Shit. I don't have my cell phone. Do you have yours?"

"On your coffee table," Jacob said as he pulled onto Main Street. He glanced into the rearview mirror. "We have company."

"Fuck," Kathleen said, her voice rising. How could he stay so calm?

He turned onto Highway 4 north and floored it.

The black car was right behind them and gaining fast. They heard the crack of gunfire and a bullet whistled past.

"Kathleen, we have to shoot him or we're dead. Use your gun."

She pulled the weapon from her belt, released the safety, rolled down the window, and fired twice. The first bullet missed and the second ricocheted off the hood with a twang.

The killer returned fire and a bullet blew out the rear windshield, shattering it.

The sound shattered Kathleen's nerves and she almost dropped the gun, pulling her arm inside to regroup mentally.

A metal crunching sound snapped both heads back as the killer slammed into the rear bumper. The SUV skidded, zigzagged along for a few seconds before Jacob wrestled control of it and jammed pedal to metal again.

The attacking vehicle had skidded out briefly after initial impact, and Jacob had managed to put a little distance between them; just enough make a hard left on Highway 3 as another bullet zinged by.

He barreled down the dark highway, plotting his next move. The black car, a newer Audi Quattro A6, was a lot faster than his SUV, and he needed to bring the chase to a terrain that would favor the SUV. *Greenfield Road up ahead*, he thought. If he could make it there, he knew some dirt roads he hoped the killer didn't know. But even if the killer did know them, Jacob was sure the rough terrain would allow them to escape. He had four-wheeled on those roads before and he knew every bump and pothole like the back of his hand.

"Greenfield Road?" It was as if Kathleen had read his mind.

"Let's hope so."

Through the rearview mirror, she saw the Quattro rapidly gaining. She was about to hang the gun out and start firing again, but suddenly saw something else. Out of nowhere, another pair of headlights appeared behind the Quattro. She blinked, not believing her eyes. Both vehicles were approaching rapidly.

"Jacob, do you see ...?"

The sound of metal smashing against metal reverberated through the interior. Her eyes widened as she realized what had happened. Black Death had just rear-ended the Quattro, and it was fishtailing out of control not fifty feet behind the SUV.

"Jacob, stop!"

"What?"

She pointed behind. He glanced at the rearview mirror and saw it. The Quattro skidded into the ditch. He slowed to a stop about a hundred yards in front of the accident. The night was dark, but they could see black silhouettes of the vehicles, headlights illuming the dark curtain of night. They exited the SUV, guns drawn. The Quattro was half in the ditch. Black Death slammed into its side, inching it forward. It teetered at a precarious angle.

The Quattro driver's door opened. The killer stepped out and fired shots at the pick-up. Black Death backed up, stopped for a second, and charged forward. The killer jumped out of the way, narrowly avoiding a transformation into road kill.

"Get in the car," Jacob said.

Kathleen obeyed and they watched the rest of the drama unfold from the SUV. Black Death repeatedly rammed the Quattro as the killer fired shots into the night. Then all was silent, but for the rumbling of Black Death's engine.

The killer, evidently tired of shooting at a driverless vehicle, had disappeared into the night.

Black Death backed up, fish-tailed a donut, and peeled away in the opposite direction. They watched as the red tail lights grew smaller, the growl of the engine growing fainter.

Jacob wasn't prepared to wait around and see if the killer would return. He was thankful to be on the bright side of the dirt—well, the starlit side, anyway. "Let's get the fuck out of here."

Chapter Eighteen

You need to get the fuck out of here, a voice inside Reggie Snyden's head said as he slowly regained consciousness later that evening. He pulled at the wrist and leg straps constricting his movements, but they wouldn't budge. He was locked in a small room in the King's County Memorial Hospital in Montague. He had been fit to be tied when he was brought in, so the staff had hospitably obliged his distemper with a complimentary gift—leather ankle and wrist straps—or bracelets, if you were fashion conscious. Staff had gone a little overboard with their generosity, securely fastening his head to the bed as well.

Doctors had removed the bullet from the flesh wound in his leg and, waking from the anesthetic, he had begun to squirm violently and growl, a low guttural sound medical officials found rather disconcerting. So they had sedated Snyden, tightened the straps, wheeled him into the room, and posted a cop at the door. He had been there just over twenty-four hours and had already overstayed his welcome.

This wasn't the red carpet treatment. Not that Snyden would realize the difference right now. The rage he had felt earlier was renewing a rapid invasion of his dulled senses, attacking a sedated head still reeling from the effects of anesthetic and morphine. He rolled his eyes from side to side, struggling again with the bracelets. They pinched his skin—the gift that keeps on giving.

As the hot rage slowly enveloped his body and mind, something else happened. The man who had morphed into a monster felt an incredible strength surge through him. He jerked his head up and snapped the strap constricting his head. He grunted, jerked both arms and snapped the other two bracelets. The monster wanted to preserve his strength—he knew he would need it for what was to come—so he untied the remaining ankle bracelets. He wasn't in a fashion conscious mood right now.

The young officer behind the door was half asleep in a chair when he first heard the growl. He opened his eyes, blinking, thinking he had been dreaming. Something about a wolf, he wasn't sure. He stood and peered through the window. Abruptly the door flew from its hinges as Snyden barreled into it. It dislodged with such violent force it knocked the officer down and landed on top of him.

And the rage, the all-consuming rage, needed to be satisfied, wouldn't be satisfied without bloodshed and death. Snyden leaped into the air and landed hard on the door, crunching it into the cop's head, once, twice, three, four, five times before the unfortunate victim finally screamed his last scream and drew his last breath. Snyden had crushed his chest and head.

Blood splattered the floor and a small red puddle spanned out around the dead man. He never had a chance.

Snyden ran down the hall, reached the nursing station, stopped and started growling ferociously, baring his teeth like a rabid wolf. Two nurses looked up, startled. One screamed—a short, shrill burst—and picked up a phone immediately while the other one, wide-eyed with fear, started backing away from the station to the medicine room, where she planned on locking herself in.

Nobody knew why Snyden didn't attack and kill the women. He certainly didn't. He was far removed from his faculties. He studied them for a few seconds—they would say later it felt like many minutes—turned, and sprinted to the stairwell, oblivious of his leg injury. He opened the door, ran down the stairs, and disappeared into the darkness.

Chapter Nineteen

When darkness turned to light, Detective Russ Willard found himself combing the woods near Drake Bellows' uni-bomber-like shack. It was a crisp, cold, sunny morning, the perfect day for a little hike. Police and detectives had scoured the area over the last few days, but had been unable to locate the infected black cat. Some other investigations, namely the pursuit of Reggie Snyden, the search for Bain Derksen, and preparation for the big opening ceremony for Casinos Inc. had pulled the police force in too many directions at once. Resources were stretched thin. So they had taken some time away from the cat hunt until after the dust settled on other pressing matters.

But not Willard. He had a point to prove. He wanted to catch the cat first, and then find Snyden, his trainee and partner. Logic said the cat had a far greater potential of infecting at a much quicker rate than Snyden. If the infected feline bit a bird, for example, and the bird got away, who knew how many other birds, how many other people it could infect? What if the cat decided to go fishing, potentially contaminating the water supply? Or what if it attacked a fox and the fox got infected? Willard had considered these dangers much more pressing than the missing Snyden. Besides, he had been told Redmond was on it. And he didn't fancy stepping on the lead detective's toes.

He wanted to be the one to make a big break in the case. The capture of the contagious animal would surely be viewed as one of the most important aspects of the case. And Willard had a need for the admiration of the masses. He had received accolades for his detective work in the past—even a promotion—and he wanted more of the same. A young and ambitious cop, he defined himself in terms of how other people viewed him—in a mirror of social acceptance. The more fans and followers he had, the greater his self-worth.

He liked to get what he wanted. And there were two things he wanted right now. One, to put himself in line for succession to the throne of Police Captain Stan Whiting. And two, an intimate and long term-relationship with Kathleen Freeborne, whom he had become attracted to during an investigation into the kidnapping of Redmond earlier in the year.

And now that her boyfriend was dead, she had become single and available. Sure, Jacob was in the way, but once she realized how shrewd of an investigator Willard was, he was sure he could win her over.

That was one of the reasons he had secretly pocketed a letter during the investigation at the Crawley residence. He had noticed a symbol of the ancient healing sword on the envelope, so he had stuffed it into his pocket, hoping it would lead to a big break in the case.

But it had turned out to be a dead end. He frowned slightly as he walked through the wooded path. A harmless letter from Crawley's daughter, Holly, who was simply keeping her dad up to date on her life—her two kids, caring husband, white picket fence in Halifax, yada-yada-yada.

The reference to the sword image on the envelope merely said: "I picked out these stickers at a dollar store and I thought they would bring you good luck."

So, with that lead dead, and the letter incinerated, Willard had focused his efforts on the stray feline. Then he would target Snyden and become the hero of PEI once again. Redmond would have to remain in the shadows for a little longer, and Willard would have some new accolades to pin to his muscular chest. Surely then Kathleen would like him. And not a Facebook like, either—he wanted the kind of like that would eventually lead to intimacy and commitment.

He heard some rustling in the woods a short distance away, stopped, and listened. He looked toward the rustling sound, but heard nothing. All he could hear were the chirping of birds, the distant and steady swoosh of the ocean waves lazily lapping at the sandy shoreline in the distance, the shhhhhhhhhhhhsshhing sound of a gentle breeze.

He walked ten feet or so. He pushed bushes back as he weaved his way along. He heard a snarl and looked up—just a little too late.

The infected black cat sprang out of a tree branch, dropped on his head, and chomped ferociously into Willard's jugular vein, simultaneously clawing at his eyes. Willard stepped back, tripping over a log, both hands clasping the throat of the demented animal.

"I've got you, you little bastard," he shouted, grunting and squeezing tighter as he fell on his back in the brush.

The cat's eyes bulged, but it dug its small fangs in deeper, piercing Willard's jugular vein. Blood spurted out like a ruptured garden hose and Willard squeezed tighter, the cat now choking as it clung onto his throat. This was no ordinary animal; otherwise the powerful detective would have easily been able to snap its neck by now. As it was, he was lying in the forest, alone and afraid, dying, as blood gushed from the punctured main artery.

With a last powerful effort, Willard twisted the cat's neck, like ringing out a wet cloth, and snapped it with a bone-cracking crunch. The fangs slowly loosened and Willard tossed the animal away.

He had killed the infected feline.

He slowly stood up, grabbing at his throat with one hand and felt for his phone with the other. It wasn't there. Must've fallen out when he fell. He wasn't prepared to look for it. He had one singular goal—get to his vehicle and drive to the hospital. One of his eyes and part of his cheek were badly gouged. He stumbled back onto the path, sat down in the mud, pulled off his shoes and a sock, which he wrapped around his bleeding neck.

He staggered along the path toward the clearing. When he was fifty feet away, he collapsed on the trail.

Townsfolk would later say Detective Russ Willard was a hero for killing the Rage Virus-infected feline.

But he was a dead hero.

Chapter Twenty

It was time. The weather had cooperated beautifully. It was a sunny Saturday afternoon: clear blue sky, a few white billowing clouds drifting by, and a temperature comfortably above freezing. Police had barricaded a part of University Avenue and Allen Street, and throngs of people mingled on the two-acre strip of land that would soon see construction of Gold Rush Casino.

A big blue tent-like gazebo sat in the middle of the lot. On it were three podiums and six chairs, where local, provincial and federal dignitaries were seated, along with Sid Baillis, his secretary, Veronica, and a few of his staff. A large red ribbon stretched in front of the gazebo, a massive pair of scissors on a table nearby.

In a corner was another blue canopy where staff served liquid refreshments: beer, wine, coffee, juice and an assortment of appetizers. Locals lined up to receive the free offerings. Still another cordoned-off cue of locals waited to receive their complimentary gold sword necklaces.

Kathleen, Redmond, and Jacob watched as Mayor Bob Boltan gave a speech, extolling the benefits Gold Rush Casino would bring to the island.

Despite the conversational drone and mutterings of the audience, Kathleen was absorbed in thought. They had narrowly escaped being killed the other night and, according to Redmond, cops had no idea who was responsible. The vehicle registration led to a dead end, there was no evidence left inside the car, and the perp had disappeared into the night. He might

115

be targeting her because of her suspicion of Sid Baillis, who sat confidently on stage next to his secretary, waiting to be introduced by the emcee.

Kathleen was also worried about the disappearance of Spike. After returning home, her beloved pet, who had saved her life, was nowhere to be found. She was saddened to learn Detective Russ Willard had been killed by the infected cat, and even though he had killed the infected animal, she still didn't believe Spike was out of harm's way.

She knew there were lots of locals who didn't follow the news. And, if they saw Spike, what would stop them from killing her and asking questions later?

And there was also the very real possibility Spike had been infected.

Adding to her worries was the troubling realization that Reggie Snyden, who had morphed into a rage-filled monster, had yet to be located by authorities. What kind of horrible violence was he was capable of? He had already killed one cop.

And what about Black Death? Redmond said the truck had been returned to the police compound, albeit with a slightly damaged front bumper and a few tell-tale black paint scars.

She knew with certainty who was driving Black Death. It was the ghost of her deceased boyfriend, still looking out for her. Things had been so crazy lately she had not tried to contact the spirits of Angela or Mark. She still wanted Angela to stop possessing her body and Mark to stop possessing Jacob's body so they could both lead normal lives, whatever that meant. With her keen psychic abilities, she doubted she could ever live a normal life. But a life with less carnage would be nice.

Finally, she was sure all of this was just the tip of the iceberg. She knew with an unexplainable certainty that things would be getting a hell of a lot worse before they got better.

She looked at Redmond, whose brow was furrowed as he concentrated on the speeches. He had his work cut out for him.

Jacob, standing at her side, wasn't looking a hundred percent either. He had told her he hadn't gotten much sleep since the attempted murder. And, when he did drift off, violent nightmares would awaken him, soaked in sweat and terrified.

Kathleen had to admit her nightmares weren't any better. Last night she had dreamed she saw a dark figure fall into a hole. She heard screams for help and ran to the hole, peering down into the darkness. But the eyes that held hers transformed fiery red and scared her. So she slammed the steel lid shut and held it while the man thrashed and screamed below. Then suddenly the voice became a familiar cry for help, and she realized grimly it was someone she knew. After a moment's thought, she jerked the lid open and the man leaped to the surface, covered in some black, slimy liquid, writhing and twisting in pain, his leg bent at an odd angle. She recognized the voice and screamed. She picked up her phone and dialed Redmond. When the detective asked her where she was, the address came to her immediately: "33 Campbell Avenue."

She abruptly woke, terrified and breathing heavily. Jacob McCreery lived at 33 Campbell Avenue.

"Are you okay?" he asked, touching her arm lightly.

She looked at him. "I wish I could say yes. But that would be a lie."

As the emcee introduced Sid Baillis, they grew quiet. Kathleen was here at Redmond's bidding, and she was being paid to detect a vibe. She wanted to hear this speech.

Baillis took the podium and cleared his throat. The crowd became silent.

"I want to thank everyone for turning up and for the warm welcome you've given me since I announced plans for Gold Rush Casino. This casino, when it's finished in a year, will create approximately 3,000 full-time jobs for Charlottetown and the surrounding area." He paused as the audience clapped.

He continued. "And I'm not counting all the local construction workers who will build it and the spin-off benefits to local suppliers. Those benefits will be huge."

More applause.

"I would also like to thank the people and politicians at the local, provincial and federal levels who have made this possible. In addition, I'd like to thank the local police, who have done an excellent job of traffic control. And thank you to everyone who has supported the venture in whatever way they could. This is a beautiful island, and the tourism is just beginning to grow. I'm sure Gold Rush Casino will serve as a great entertainment venue for locals and tourists alike."

With that he stepped down the stairs and, with the help of the city mayor, picked up the large scissors. As cameras flashed and flicked, they cut the red ribbon.

Applause broke out and slowly subsided.

"I won't bore you with any more talk," Baillis said. "You've already heard from local politicians."

The crowd laughed.

"Go and enjoy yourselves," Baillis said after the laughter had subsided. "Eat, drink and be merry. And don't forget the free gold necklaces."

"Are you going to stay?" Kathleen said, looking at Redmond and Jacob. She didn't know which one of them she was asking.

Redmond shook his head. "I've got work to do. Unless I find Snyden by the end of today, health officials are going to declare an epidemic. We're going to have to go public with this. And that's not what politicians want right now."

"I'm going home," Jacob said, looking sick to his stomach. "I don't feel like drinking and I'm not hungry, anyway." His expression was forlorn.

He said his goodbyes and disappeared through the maze of people.

Redmond pulled Kathleen out of earshot of the masses. "Can you enlighten me at all?"

"Other than to tell you I think this is the tip of the iceberg, no, I can't. I wish I could tell you more."

"No vibe whatsoever?"

"Nothing strong enough to be able to explain anything."

"Do you see anyone you recognize?"

She searched the crowd while the detective watched her silently. She shook her head.

"Do you want to stick around?" She had come with Redmond and didn't have readily available transport for the return trip to Montague.

"No. I want to find Spike."

"I'll drop you off."

She nodded and they walked across the street, leaving the revelers to enjoy the festivities and take advantage of the free necklaces, the same necklaces that would later be described as "the curse of Prince Edward Island."

Chapter Twenty-One

Anne Gruneld woke up the next morning feeling angry and cursed. She looked at her plump facial features in the mirror and cringed. But she didn't know if she would rather be skinny. Right now, she didn't know what she wanted. Her eyes moved down to the gold necklace around her neck and even that didn't bring a smile to her face. She didn't know why, but she didn't want to take it off, either.

She brushed her teeth, splashed some water on her face, and ran a comb through her short blond hair. Normally she would shower every morning, but not today. *If people don't like me the way I am, then fuck them,* she thought. That thought and the attitude that went with it were usually foreign to Anne. She was opinionated and if she believed in something strongly enough, she would vigorously defend her position. But "fuck them"? That was a little harsh, even for her.

She dressed and walked into the living room, where Rusty Sales was flaked out on the couch, channel-surfing. They had a good relationship, for the most part. One of the very few knocks Anne had on her construction worker boyfriend was he could be a little lazy at times. But hell, no one was perfect, right? It was Sunday, after all, so why should she bother giving him a hard time?

But the hostility invading her body and mind wouldn't allow any alternatives.

"Did you have a good sleep, baby?" Rusty said, finally deciding on an NFL football game and setting the remote down. He was not prepared for what would come next.

"Why don't you take your lazy ass off the couch for once in your life," she said angrily, balling her fists and glaring at him. If looks could kill.

There was a moment's pause. Rusty looked stunned. "Wow ... who shit in your cornflakes this morning?"

Without saying a single word, she stormed out of the house, slamming the door behind her so hard the noise reverberated loudly throughout the living room where Rusty had planned a leisurely and uneventful day.

She didn't notice the hostile vibe on the streets as she stormed through the downtown core. There were angry people everywhere, some vehemently arguing, others raising their fists and shouting.

And still others squaring off in toe-to-toe fistfights.

Three hours later—and exactly twenty-four hours from when she had first put the necklace on—she returned home in an uncontrollable rage, an infected rage.

Rusty was snoring loudly on the couch. She walked into the kitchen, picked out the biggest carving knife she could find, returned to the living room and stabbed him through the throat, burying the knife to the hilt.

Blood spurted out as he opened his eyes in terror, gurgled, and gasped. She stepped back, appreciating her handy work, enjoying the close-up view of his body twitching with spasms before becoming motionless.

She returned to the kitchen, armed herself with some cutlery, and left the house.

In search of her next victim.

Chapter Twenty-Two

I don't want to be the next victim, Kathleen thought, hearing the wailing of sirens growing louder, watching people march zombie-like down the street. She slammed the front door as a wild-eyed man cast a menacing glance and started toward her house.

"Here," Jacob said, handing her a gun.

She took it nervously and searched his troubled eyes. They rushed into the living room and peered out the bay window. A vehicle driving down the street had distracted an infected man and he turned and marched toward it resolutely. The vehicle accelerated and slammed into him, sending him flipping into the air, tumbling off the hood. He lay motionless as it careened down the street, swerving occasionally to bump off oncoming rage-filled zombies.

"Where's Redmond?" Jacob asked.

"I called him earlier. He should be here soon."

She had seen the carnage in a horrific nightmare last night and snapped bolt upright at 7:30 am this morning trembling with fear and sweat-soaked. Infected people, zombies, were parading around the town, killing at random. Some were armed, and others attacked en masse, overwhelming their victims and biting them, tearing off huge chunks of flesh. As events of the nightmare flooded her mind, she knew with an eerie certainty it was more than just a nightmare. It was a psychic vision, and it would all be coming very true very soon.

So she had hurriedly dressed, called Redmond, who had told her the police station was being overrun by zombies and he had his hands full. But he planned on retreating to a small cottage he owned fronting Poverty Beach, and he promised to rescue them.

The second panicked call was to Jacob. He didn't hesitate to drive over. He knew if Kathleen said so, that a violent wave of carnage was on its way. It was cresting and would soon sweep down on the unsuspecting town with an unspeakable fury.

"Did you check the back door?" Kathleen said, panic rising in her voice.

"I did."

"And it's locked?"

"Yeah."

"I think you should keep watch there. I'll watch the front."

"Okay." Jacob disappeared down the hall.

Kathleen ducked behind the curtain of the bay window, trying to keep her head out of view. If they didn't see her, maybe they wouldn't come. No point in giving them a reason.

She glanced around the room and saw a black paw under the couch. She sighed. At least her cat was back. After Redmond had dropped her off yesterday, she had begun searching the neighborhood for Spike. Returning about an hour later, she saw Spike sitting on the front porch, meowing her I-want-attention meow.

"How's it going back there?" she shouted.

"I don't see anyone."

"Stay there anyway."

"Okay."

A wide-eyed zombie suddenly stopped right in front of the house, his attention caught by the fluttering of the bay window curtain. Kathleen had accidentally brushed her hand against it.

Shit. He's coming. She ran to the front door and watched him stumble up the walk, hands outstretched, eyes far away.

"JACOB!"

"Yeah."

"Someone's coming up the walkway."

He ran to the front door, just as the zombie arrived. The zombie growled, then punched his fist through the small window and started groping for the deadbolt.

Jacob pointed the gun and shot him in the head. The zombie dropped dead on the porch, infected blood and brain matter dribbling down his forehead. The gunshot caught the attention of two more. They veered off and headed toward the house.

"We're going to have to shoot them," Jacob said.

Kathleen leveled her piece and fired three times. The first bullet missed, but the other two connected, one to the head of each zombie. They fell off the porch with a thud and hit the ground dead.

But more were coming.

Her phone rang. It was Redmond. "I'm on my way. I have to pick up Jeanette first, then I'll get you."

"Hurry. They're swarming the front door."

Jacob fired off two more shots, killing two more zombies on the porch. But the crack of gunfire was attracting attention, and more were slowly plodding over.

Then something inexplicable happened. Black Death barreled up the street, its engine roaring loudly, knocking off zombies as it neared. The truck crashed through the white picket fence bordering the front lawn, plowing over four zombies in the process, and skidded to a stop a few feet from the porch.

The driver door opened and a man stepped out, calmly ushering them forward. Kathleen saw him but could barely believe it. "Do you see that?"

"Black Death, yeah. I see Black Death."

"No, Mark?"

Jacob shook his head.

Kathleen looked again and saw the apparition of Mark Riley smile and fade away.

"Let's go," she said. It took a few minutes for her to pack some belongings and finally coax Spike into the small cat cage. When everything was packed, she stood at the front door with Jacob. They looked at each other for a split second, acknowledged their readiness to depart, and Jacob pushed it open. Chased by zombies, they darted to the truck, jumping over bodies and outstretched arms. They climbed in hurriedly, Kathleen at the wheel.

More zombies approached from the rear, trying to hitch a ride. She slammed it into reverse, backed over them, stopped, slammed into drive, and floored it down the side street, swerving to avoid corpses and the aimless wanderings of those with the mission to kill and infect. Kathleen didn't want to kill them unless she absolutely had to, in case a cure could be found.

While they drove through the macabre landscape, Jacob called Redmond, informing him of a slight change in plans. They would meet at Redmond's cottage by the beach.

A little while later, they rolled up to the isolated cottage. The one-and-a-half story home sat on three manicured acres and fronted the ocean in a secluded fashion. The closest neighbor was a good city block away. The cottage was strategically positioned with an unobstructed view of the ocean in the front and backed onto a large field with very little brush and clear sightlines—exactly what they needed right now. They would be able to see their attackers and pick them off long before they got close. At least that was the hope.

Two zombies stood drunkenly on the porch, peering in the bay window as Black Death came to a stop.

Distracted by the noise, the zombies lumbered toward Black Death, arms outstretched.

Jacob exited, gun drawn. He looked at Kathleen for a sign. She nodded and he stepped forward, firing. After two misses, one bullet finally struck a zombie in the face and the other zombie was the unlucky recipient of a bullet between the eyes.

They dropped dead.

Jacob walked onto the porch, extracted a house key from underneath a welcome mat, opened the door, and entered. Kathleen followed, carrying Spike and a duffle bag.

Redmond pulled up in his black Crown Vic, Jeanette in the passenger seat. Her short brown hair was matted to the side of her face, her eyes bloodshot. She had been crying.

Redmond helped Jeanette out of the car and supported her with an arm around her waist as he escorted her inside. She walked into the living room and sat down. He quickly introduced Jeanette to Kathleen and Jacob and then retreated to his Crown Vic, popped the trunk open, and retrieved a large cache of weapons, which he brought into the house. He returned to the door, glanced around, and locked it quickly.

"Kathleen, stay here with Jeanette," Redmond said. "Jacob, come with me."

Jacob stood. The detective pulled two rifles and two AK-47s from his duffle bag, handed a rifle to Jacob, and they went upstairs. In the upstairs hallway, he said: "Check the front bedroom by the ocean and I'll look out here."

Jacob peered out in all directions. "I can't see anyone."

"Good," Redmond said, satisfied. The coast was clear on his end as well. They went downstairs and sat with the women. Kathleen had released Spike from the cage, put some food out for her, and sat next to Jeanette on the couch. She held her hand. The terrified comforting the terrified. Someone had to hold it together.

After a quick lesson in weapons handling and some instruction on how the guard posts would be organized, Redmond finally sat down with the others and explained his theories.

"It's only a matter of time before the military gets involved. So what we want to do is stay put. If we go wandering around outside, we might get mistaken for zombies and shot and killed."

"Are there any clues as to the origin of this virus?" Kathleen asked.

Jacob picked up an AK-47 and went to the front door while they talked. He wasn't taking any chances. The detective searched his eyes as he returned. Jacob shook his head and Redmond continued.

"Well, we have our suspicions, but nothing has been proven."

Kathleen was sure Baillis was somehow behind it all, but she had no solid evidence. And did it really matter right now, anyway? Their first priority was survival. "What about a cure?"

"That's where I do have some news," Redmond said. "Politicians have recruited the services of a pharmaceutical company in Halifax to try and come up with a vaccination and a cure. They're working with the blood of the first known victim, Jonathon Crawley."

"Any idea on time frame?" Jeanette asked. She had wiped her teary eyes with some tissue and had done her best to try and compose herself. But her hands still trembled, her face an ashen-white.

"I don't know," Redmond said. "I'm in contact with the police captain. He's been flown to Halifax, out of harm's way, along with local politicians and other dignitaries."

"Why didn't they take us?" Kathleen said.

"There was no time. It was all they could do to get out. We just have to wait."

"Yeah, for how long?" Jeanette asked, her voice tinged with panic. "We're being attacked by fucking infected zombies. This is right out of a horror movie."

"I don't know, honey. I'm supposed to get an update later tonight. In the meantime, we have to try and stay calm, hunker down, and stay alert."

"Would anyone like some tea?" Kathleen asked. She didn't know what else to say.

They nodded and she disappeared into the kitchen, reappearing a few minutes later with a tray with four cups, some condiments, and a hot, steeping teapot. She set it down on the coffee table.

Kathleen knew there was something Redmond had forgotten in his speech about staying calm. He had forgotten to say they would also have to kill infected zombies before the zombies killed them.

"We've got incoming," Jacob said from his post at the door.

Redmond grabbed his rifle and ran to the door. Two staggering bodies, male and female, lumbered through the field, probably seventy-five feet away. Redmond went to a side window in the living room, popped it open, trained his rifle—crack, crack—and brought down the pair with head shots.

Spike, who had been curiously watching from underneath an armchair, meowed and darted upstairs.

"There," Redmond said. "Now we can drink our tea in peace."

"Just another day in zombie-land," Kathleen said.

In spite of themselves, they all laughed, a mechanism to release the nervous tension in the air.

"Here," Redmond said, waving a pack of cigars in front of Jacob. He knew the women didn't smoke. "Want one?"

"Sure." Jacob took one, lit it, and took a few deep drags. Redmond popped another window open in the living room, lit up, and joined Jacob by the window while Kathleen and Jeanette chatted nervously on the couch.

Redmond didn't want to show it in his expression, but he didn't have a clue how long they might have to wait around before help arrived. He did have a plan B. There was a speedboat anchored to the dock floating in the water. If they had to, they could use it and escape to one of the smaller islands a short distance away. Either way, he knew it was going to be a long night. He anxiously awaited the call from Captain Whiting.

As if reading his mind, Jacob said, "I don't feel that good about spending the night here."

Chapter Twenty-Three

That night, eight officials sat in an ornate office around an oval table in a government building in Halifax discussing the Rage Virus epidemic on Prince Edward Island.

In attendance were Police Captain Stan Whiting, Rex Robertson, scientist at Ovrex Pharmaceuticals, Charlottetown Mayor Bob Boltan, PEI Premier Les Simon, Elisa Stewart, a disease control expert from the Public Health Agency of Canada, and Canadian Forces General Marty Stanner.

Elisa brushed back her long blond hair, studied her notepad, and addressed Rex. "You say you have a cure for this virus? How can you have one so fast? And how can you be sure it works?"

"Let me explain," the beady-eyed bald man said, removing his glasses and setting them down. "As soon as it was discovered Jonathon Crawley had a virus, your government contacted us to begin analyzing it. We discovered fairly quickly it was very similar in nature to the Swine Flu, which we have discovered not only a cure for, but a vaccination for as well. So, we ran a trial, injected one of our lab animals with the virus and, after he became infected, injected him with a variation of the Swine Flu cure. Two days later, he recovered. Additionally, we inoculated one of the monkeys with the vaccine, and later injected him with the virus. So far, he hasn't shown any symptoms."

Something didn't feel right to Elisa; first, a deadly virus and soon after a cure and vaccination. She didn't trust this man. The whole thing reeked of more than government involvement. It smacked of a government conspiracy. But she couldn't prove any of it. And she also knew there was a lot of pressure to get this mess cleared up as soon as possible. Lots of people were dying and there was the very real possibility of it spreading to the mainland, if it hadn't already.

Before she could respond, Premier Les Simon said: "Let's say this cure does work. How do you propose we administer this?"

General Marty Stanner responded. "It's my understanding that the military would have to play a key role. But it isn't going to be pretty. We're looking at containment first, then eliminating active carriers and inoculating the remainder of the island population. From there health officials would see to the inoculation of the rest of the country."

The premier scratched his chin, darting his intelligent brown eyes around the room. There was silence. He was in charge. The decisions he made—for better or worse—would be his legacy. "Are you telling me you have to kill all those carriers before you can inoculate the island population? Can't you tranquilize them or something?"

The general cleared his throat. "Sir, we have the Confederation Bridge, the only land exit route from the island, sealed off with military force. We've tried tranquilizer darts on carriers trying to breach the border. They have no effect whatsoever. And we don't have time for research. We have to contain, eliminate and inoculate."

"How is containment going?" Charlottetown Mayor Bob Boltan asked. A bead of sweat sprouted on his brow.

"As I said, the land exit is sealed, the ferry system shut down. Boats, planes and choppers are patrolling the coastline," Stanner said. "Right now, no one can get off the island."

"What about the people who are trapped there but not infected?" Elisa asked. "They're at the mercy of the zombies?"

"Before we can free them, we have to kill all the active carriers," Stanner said matter-of-factly. "And there are a lot."

Police Captain Stan Whiting was growing impatient. He had been told choppers would be coming in right away to remove his men. He had promised Redmond he would have him and his friends airlifted to safety in less than twenty-four hours. Now he would have to stall the man. And it was unclear if a rescue would even be attempted, never mind when. The sacrifice of a few for the greater good of the many.

"Wait a fucking minute, here," the police captain said, his face reddening. "I was told you'd have military choppers in there immediately to get my men. Fuck, I've still got officers stranded in police stations fighting these carriers off. I promised them I'd have them airlifted within twenty-four hours. Now you're telling me you're going to attack the island and, when you think you've killed all the fucking zombies, you'll have people come in with fucking hazmat suits and inoculate the survivors?"

The general remained stone-faced. "Our first efforts must be concentrated on containment, sir, before we can look at rescue."

"Excuse me," Elisa said. All heads turned toward her. "I presume I can speak candidly here, and we can cut the bullshit." She didn't wait for an acknowledgement. "It seems to me something is missing in this entire plan, unless I'm missing something."

Elisa checked her notes before continuing. "Somehow, it seems to have been forgotten here that this virus started with an infected cat. Who's to say a good part of the animal population hasn't been infected already? What about birds, or ocean life, or water supplies? You plan on killing all the zombies, sure. What about the birds that may have spread the virus already? What about the other animals?" She looked at Rex, as if he had the answer.

"We haven't had time to run trials on birds," Rex said. "It's possible they might be immune. And we know the virus has yet to mutate and develop the capacity to spread airborne. We also know it won't survive in water. It's doubtful fish or water supplies are contaminated or would become contaminated."

"'Doubtful,'" Elisa said, her eyes narrowing to slits. "That's all you can say is 'doubtful'?"

"At this stage, until more tests can be done, yes," Rex said.

"She still has a point," the premier said, growing impatient. He had an epidemic on his hands and it seemed they were hardly close to implementing a plan. Lives were being lost, his political career hanging in the balance. "We need a plan that calls for more than just killing off the infected. What about the animals and birds?"

There was a long silence. There was a solution emerging that the premier didn't like the sounds of—nuke the entire island. There had to be a better way. "Listen, will you run some trials on the other animal species?"

Rex nodded.

Mayor Bob Bolton remained quiet, smearing a napkin over his sweaty brow.

The premier continued: "Okay, first on the list are birds. Find out if they're immune, and report your findings to my deputy immediately. Then go through the various indigenous animals. Thankfully there aren't a lot of species there. I think right now we have to act on the supposition the virus cannot infect birds, water supplies, or sea life. If we find out it can infect other species, once the population is immune, we should be able to deal with it."

He paused for a moment while he thought. "Tell me, Rex, could you put this cure into a tranquilizer dart, put it in a gun and use it to shoot an infected animal?"

"I don't see why not," Rex said. "It's been done before. It just takes time for it to take effect."

"Why can't you do that with the infected humans?" the police captain said. "Instead of shooting them?"

"Right now the primary goal is containment," the general said. "The cure, if it even works, will take far too long. In the meantime, the zombies are killing and infecting other civilians."

"So we shoot the humans and save the animals?" Elisa said.

"I don't see another option," General Stanner said. "Some will have to die for the sake of the greater good." He turned to the premier. "On my end, sir, I need your orders? In conjunction with the containment phase, do we proceed with elimination as top priority—then proceed with rescue and inoculation?"

Captain Whiting bristled. "I want my fucking men removed."

"I'm sorry," Mayor Bob Bolton said. "It looks like we have more important priorities."

Captain Whiting was furious. He glared at the mayor. "You're the fucking mayor and you're telling me it's not top priority to save your constituents? Where's your fucking head ...?"

"That's enough," the premier interrupted. "We have work to do. And we don't have a lot of time." He stood up to leave. "General, go ahead with elimination and containment. And keep me closely apprised. Elisa, I want you to work with Rex on the virus trials."

He turned to Captain Whiting. "I'm sorry, Stan. We'll get your men. It's just going to take a little more time. For now I want you working closely with military officials. Give them what they want. And don't raise any shit in the process. The rest of you—you know what your jobs are. Do them!"

The meeting was over.

The premier left the office and the others slowly stood up. It had been a three-hour session, and before the virus would be contained and eliminated, many local residents would have to be killed.

Mayor Bob Bolton waited until he arrived in the lobby of the downtown Holiday Inn before he allowed himself a smile. Everything was going according to plan. When this was all over, he was going to be a rich man.

Chapter Twenty-Four

Rex Robertson was going to be a rich man. He rubbed his hands together and grinned as he picked up the phone in his office. He was daydreaming about what he'd do with all the money once the drugs were distributed world-wide. He knew one thing for sure. He wouldn't have to work another day in his life—even if he was just turning sixty and still had a lot of energy. Hell, he would use it to live out his lascivious fantasies on an island somewhere in the Caribbean.

He already knew the Rage Virus, his brainchild, wouldn't contaminate water or fish. And he was 99 percent sure birds were immune to it. That would have to be enough.

He just couldn't release the results too early for fear of being discovered.

His experimental monkey had reacted perfectly to the virus, the subsequent cure, the inoculation, and another injection of the virus. He was as healthy as ever, as cheerful as a caged laboratory animal could be. He knew he would soon have some human test subjects.

But that Elisa Stewart had been asking a lot of questions. Oh well. If she got in the way, there was always Bain, who was stationed nearby in case anything got out of hand. He hoped the use of Bain's deadly force wouldn't be necessary. If it was, at least not until long after Rex had disappeared. He had his escape plan and fake identities all in order. This had been in the planning stages for nearly two years. Truth be told, he didn't trust Bain or Baillis. But, for now, he needed them.

Needed the big pay-off from Baillis, the secret owner of Ovrex Pharmaceuticals. Needed Bain if things got a little dicey.

He had one more call to make before he would permit himself a celebratory shot of whiskey. He picked up the phone. Sid Baillis answered. "How did it go?"

"Like clockwork."

"Any problems you can foresee?"

"Elisa Stewart is a little suspicious. She might pose a problem."

"Are you working with her on the trials?"

"Yes."

"Keep a close eye on her. If you think she's on to us, let me know immediately."

"Will do."

Baillis hung up and Rex finally reached for Jack Daniels. He was a man of inexpensive tastes.

But he knew that would change when he received his ten million dollars.

Chapter Twenty-Five

Five million dollars. That was how much Charlottetown Mayor Bob Bolton would get from Sid Baillis for helping to facilitate the implementation of the Rage Virus, the subsequent cure, and inoculation. He had helped to implement the plan almost seamlessly. Authorities were buying it hook, line, and sinker.

Lying on his king-sized bed in the Holiday Inn, channel-surfing, admiring his formidable pot-belly, sipping a glass of Glenlivet Scotch, he made a mental checklist of existing obstacles: Kathleen Freeborne, Detective Blaine Redmond, Jacob McCreery, Captain Stan Whiting and disease control expert Elisa Stewart.

Freeborne, McCreery and Redmond shouldn't be a problem. Baillis had a man on the inside, a Sergeant Dan Maloney from the Canadian Forces who had promised to take them out for a measly five hundred thousand. Oh well. Dan was the one with the gambling addiction, the alcohol and relationship problems. And Dan thought the money would fix all that. Maybe it would. Maybe it wouldn't. But it wasn't Bolton's problem anymore. Redmond, Freeborne and McCreery were trapped on the island, soon to come to an untimely end, compliments of the Canadian military.

He settled on *Madison County,* a dismally-contrived and poorly-scripted horror movie, set the remote down, took a sip of scotch, and returned to his thoughts. He had already taken care of his cheating wife, Debra, thanks to the Rage Virus and the infected sword necklace she had been so eager to receive.

The bitch had been cheating on him for over two years. He hadn't said anything. He had planned on surprising her after his political term expired and then divorcing her. But after Baillis approached him, it made a lot more sense for Debra to receive a tainted sword necklace, become an infected zombie, and die either by uninfected citizens defending their lives or well-aimed bullets from the Canadian military. He knew if she wasn't dead yet, she soon would be.

He smiled at the thought, took another sip of the expensive scotch, and thought about the others: Elisa Stewart and Police Captain Stan Whiting. Both had seemed a little too curious for comfort.

He would have to talk to Baillis.

Was he forgetting anyone? What about that lawyer, Lori Bellafonte? There was something about her he didn't trust. He knew she was still on the island. And, as far as he knew, she hadn't been infected, at least not by the tainted necklace, anyway. Bolton knew Baillis had gifted her an untainted necklace in order to exploit her talents a little longer. She could be dead right now, for all he knew. But he wanted to make sure all loose ends were tied up, nothing left to chance.

He stood up, brushed his comb-over in place, went to the bathroom and relieved himself.

About a half hour and four neat scotches later, thoughts of the loose ends were swirling in his mind, starting to replace his earlier calm with unease. He wasn't even paying attention to *Madison County*. He wasn't missing much. He staggered to the hotel phone, picked it up, and dialed Sid Baillis.

Baillis picked up on the first ring. He was furious. "What the fuck are you doing? I told you never to call me on a landline. You're using the fucking hotel land line." Bolton had a disposable phone reserved strictly for communication with Baillis. But, in his alcohol-induced state, he had forgotten all about it.

"Sorry," he said in a slightly slurred voice. "I just want to make sure you've got Whiting, Stewart and Bella ..." The line went dead.

Two minutes later, his cell phone rang. He picked it up. It was Baillis, considerably calmer. "Sorry about earlier. I think you have a point. Let's talk face-to-face. Can you meet me in an hour at the pub across the street from your hotel?"

Bolton hesitated. He didn't care for Baillis on a personal level. The relationship was strictly business.

"I want to talk about a bonus," Baillis said.

That decided it for Bolton. He agreed.

"Bring your phone. I want to replace it," Baillis said before hanging up.

An hour later, Mayor Bob Bolton thought his appearance was suitably dapper as he stood on the main street, waiting for a break in traffic. He was dressed in a neatly-pressed black suit, starched white shirt, and a red tie. He could have been attending a funeral. The last car passed and he started walking. He was jaywalking, but what the hell. It was late. Nobody would notice.

As Bolton reached the middle of the intersection, Bain Derksen started the engine of the black, untraceable vehicle, shoulder-checked and pulled out. He slowed as he neared the rotund pedestrian, checked the rearview mirror, and rolled to a stop. He rolled down the window.

"Sir," he said in a convincing lost-tourist voice. "Can you please tell me how to get to the main highway from here?"

Bolton turned around, opened his mouth to speak, and was shot twice in the head with a silenced weapon.

He dropped dead in the middle of the road.

Bain smiled, rolled up the window, and drove away. *Too easy, but I still can't wait to get out of here.*

Chapter Twenty-Six

We're never going to get out of here, Kathleen thought. *Don't think like that. Glass half full, remember. Calm waters.* But she was having a hard time seeing that view right now, armed with a loaded AK-47, standing in the living room and looking out the bay window with Redmond while Jacob and Jeanette slept upstairs. They were, after all, in a fight for their lives with fucking zombies. Right out of a movie, but none-the-less here she was killing zombies. She had already shot six zombies. Riddled them with machine gun fire and watched them drop dead.

And the rescue chopper Redmond had promised hadn't arrived. Redmond had just gotten off the phone with Police Captain Stan Whiting, who had told him the first objective of the military was containment and elimination. That meant before they would even think about rescue, they would have to kill all the zombies. How long would that take? Kathleen had no idea, but she suspected the military would target the heavily populated areas first, before reaching the sparsely populated rural areas. Fuck. That was not what she wanted to hear right now.

She sat down on the couch, set her AK-47 on the coffee table, and put her hands to her face. A few tears rolled down her cheeks. She quickly wiped them away with her shirtsleeve. *Hold up there girl. You are floating on a cloud, the master of your soul. Your friends need you right now. Don't be miserable. Misery only breeds more misery.*

Redmond watched her from his post at the bay window, not knowing what to say. His plan called for them to stay put until the military arrived, and that plan was fraught with life-threatening obstacles, obstacles he knew were fast becoming too much for this emotional, anxious and sensitive woman sitting in front of him.

He sat beside her. "Are you okay?"

She slowly nodded. "When do you think they'll come for us?"

"I don't know. Whiting figured it would take a week or more to reach containment."

"Do you want to hang around here for another week?"

"I've been trying to think of different options. The Confederation Bridge is sealed, the ferry service shut down. And if we take my boat we risk accidental—or intentional—death by the military. I'm told they're vigorously patrolling the waterways."

"Yeah, but I've got a bad feeling about hanging around here."

"What, like a vision?"

"Not yet, but I've been puzzling over some of the pieces and I think the danger we're in extends beyond the zombies."

This was becoming obvious to Detective Redmond, but he had tried to downplay it. They had enough immediate problems to deal with. But he knew the mass infection had started after the ground-breaking ceremony, which somehow led to Baillis. And, although he couldn't prove it yet, he was sure the hitman sent to kill Kathleen and Jacob was also the work of Baillis. The CEO knew about Kathleen's psychic abilities and would view her as an obstacle that needed to be eliminated. Hell, for all he knew, Baillis was targeting him as well. Maybe that was why they were still stranded on the island. And didn't Whiting say something about a cure that was being developed by a pharmaceutical company? For all Redmond knew, Baillis was behind that too. Maybe this was all about money? Even Kathleen's psychic feeling about Baillis pointed to his involvement. When you added it all up, it became highly conceivable that Baillis would want them all dead. They were in his way.

"I agree," Redmond said finally.

"And I think I know how he infected all those people."

This surprised Redmond. He hadn't yet assembled all the pieces, particularly since they were in a life and death struggle with zombies right now. "You do?"

"The necklaces."

Redmond digested the information. He wished he had come to the conclusion first, but nevertheless, had to admit she was probably right. It added up.

"Think about it," Kathleen said. "The mass infection started right after all those people got those necklaces. I bet if you check those corpses outside, you'll find they're all wearing them."

"Wait here." He grabbed a flashlight, slung the machine gun over his shoulder, and left. It was windy and chilly. The sky had turned crimson red, announcing the breaking of a new day. They had pulled an all-night vigil.

He carefully checked the corpses, noticing gold sword necklaces on five of the six victims. The dead body with no necklace could be explained. It could have easily been someone who had been infected by a necklace-wearing zombie. He kicked the victim over and examined the body closer. There were teeth marks in the right hand, a chunk of flesh missing.

"Fuck," he said into the dawn, running into the house. Things had happened so fast, he hadn't had a chance to connect the dots.

Kathleen had resumed guard position at the window, AK-47 at the ready, searching the perimeter for signs of activity. She could hear stirrings from upstairs. The others were waking up.

Redmond bristled. "You're right. I need to make a phone call."

A sleepy-eyed Jacob walked down the stairs, followed by an equally sleepy-eyed Jeanette.

"What's going on?" he asked as Redmond dialed Police Captain Stan Whiting. Kathleen motioned for Jacob to sit down and explained.

Jeanette wandered into the kitchen to make breakfast.

The captain picked up on the first ring.

"We have a problem here sir," Redmond said.

"Fucking right we have a problem."

What was the captain talking about?

"Mayor Bob Bolton was murdered last night, execution-style. Definitely a professional job."

Redmond digested the news. Maybe Bolton was in on it? Imagine how much money he stood to make if a cure and inoculation for the Rage Virus was distributed world-wide? There were millions, probably billions of dollars at stake.

"Sir, we've traced the infection to the necklaces Baillis distributed at the ground-breaking ceremony. I've identified five victims wearing them."

"Redmond, those necklaces were commercially available before Baillis handed them out."

"Sir, I also recognized three of the victims from the ground-breaking ceremony. I think it's worth checking out. And why was the mayor suddenly killed? Maybe he was in on it and dropped the ball."

There was a pause. "Okay, I'm on it."

"One more thing captain."

Whiting was growing impatient. "What?"

"I think Baillis is coming after us. We know too much, and he had a bad feeling about Kathleen. I could see it in his eyes when we interviewed him." That was a slip.

"You interviewed him? I told you to stay the fuck away from him."

"Sorry sir. Anyway … get us out of here, and fast. I don't trust Baillis."

Another long pause. "I'm sorry, I can't do that. My hands are tied right now. The military is taking over. They fucking pulled rank on us. How many other men do you think I've got fighting for their lives over there?"

Redmond could hear the choppers now, rotors thumping in the distance, growing louder. Were they coming to rescue or kill them? He didn't know. But he was going to find out. "I have to go … there are incoming choppers … Please help us!"

A chopper landed in the field nearby. Six military men disembarked quickly, stealthily moving toward the house armed with assault rifles, led by one man.

The chopper sat idling.

The detective shouted orders to the group, distributing arms.

Wait a minute. Where was Jeanette? He ran into the kitchen and noticed the back door was open. She had slipped out.

He went after her.

Jeanette had heard the chopper from the beach, ran around to the front, and was now walking toward the assault team with her hands up.

"No," Kathleen shouted from the door. "Jeanette, come back!"

Redmond saw it happen just as he reached the front lawn. When Jeanette was within six feet of the approaching assault team, there was a short burst of machine gun fire. The lead man sprayed a row of bullets across the chest of her sheer white nightgown.

She screamed—a short, shrill burst—and dropped dead in front of her husband.

Jacob ran to Redmond's side as the cracking sound of machine gun fire erupted—short staccato bursts. Redmond was filled with rage. And it was not infected rage. He started to sprint toward the murderer, when Jacob shouted at him: "GET INSIDE NOW OR YOU'LL GET KILLED!"

The survival instinct seemed to override the detective's death wish and need for vengeance, at least for the time being. His hate-filled eyes registered some semblance of normalcy. Just a flash, but enough to get him to scramble for cover inside the house and narrowly avoid getting killed.

Kathleen was already upstairs, her weapon pointed out the window and spraying bullets at the team, which was surrounding them. Kathleen shot and killed two of the trailing men. The remaining men fanned out around the property.

Redmond and Jacob were downstairs in the heat of a firefight.

"Stay here," Redmond ordered Jacob, sprinting to the back door. He heard Kathleen firing her weapon from upstairs. To the rattling of machine gun fire, the detective approached the back door, diving to the floor and sliding into the kitchen wall. He popped to his knees, pointed his weapon out a broken window, and shot a soldier attempting to enter from the back. The soldier had a tear gas canister in his hand and was preparing to pull the pin and toss it inside before he was killed.

Redmond saw his chance and took it. He kicked the door open, spraying bullets as he exited. Another soldier charged toward the house, armed with a grenade. Redmond cut the man down, grabbed the fallen grenade, flung it to the ocean, and hit the dirt. It exploded in mid-air with a thunderous boom.

How many down? He didn't know. He jumped up, ran to the front of the house, and stopped abruptly. Two soldiers were being attacked by a multitude of zombies—four or five zombies to each soldier—and more were slowly lumbering forward. They bit into their victims, growling angrily and tearing large chunks of flesh from their limbs.

Redmond retreated to the back door, entered the house, locked it securely, and ran into the living room. They watched the helicopter fly away as the assault team was gruesomely murdered, limbs, flesh and bone savagely ripped away piece by piece.

"Hold your fire," Redmond said to Kathleen. She couldn't stand the horrific, blood-curdling screams of the dying and wanted to put everyone out of their misery. They were as good as dead anyway.

She stopped, eyeballing the detective. Was he still sane? She spun around, away from the macabre spectacle, and sat on the couch, trying to slow her rapid breathing. She couldn't believe she hadn't had a single anxiety attack during all this bloodshed. Although she had come awfully close, within inches really, the debilitating anxiety had never manifested itself. The need to fight to survive had overtaken the flight response.

Jacob and Redmond stood at the bay window, machine guns leveled at the murderous spectacle on the lawn. Redmond seemed to be enjoying it.

When they could see the soldiers lying on the ground, now completely overpowered by the zombies, Redmond finally gave the order: "NOW!"

They fired, spraying bullets and mowing down the crazed flesh eaters.

Chapter Twenty-Seven

By early evening, a crazed Redmond was half in the bag. He had pulled out a bottle of vodka, started off by mixing it with fruit juice, and a few hours later was drinking straight from the bottle. Kathleen held a glass of wine, her second of the night.

Jacob had gotten into the beer and, while not totally wasted, he had a nice buzz going.

They had tried calling Captain Whiting earlier but had not been able to get through. No cell signal. Perhaps the military had cut the services to prevent unauthorized escape?

They sat in the living room around a raging fire Redmond had started. He had claimed Jeanette loved sitting around the fireplace in the evening and they were going to have a fire in her memory—a wake of sorts. "She would have wanted that," the detective had said, igniting the blaze and returning to his vodka.

"You know, she was the one who kept me together," Redmond said, eyeing his houseguests with wild and faraway eyes.

Kathleen wasn't prepared to rain on the detective's parade. The man had just lost his wife. He had a right to grieve. And get pissed, if that's what he wanted to do. She was worried, though, that at any minute he might decide to bring the corpse of his wife indoors to join in a macabre celebration. He was looking so out of his mind right now he might even decide to put a drink in her dead hand.

"To Jeanette," she said, raising her glass with an unsteady hand.

Jacob held up his beer can.

The detective, slumped in an armchair, rose on unsteady legs and clinked his bottle. "To Jeanette, the love of my love ... I mean my life. She was the best wife I could've ever asked for. May she find happiness wherever she went."

"Cheers," Jacob and Kathleen said simultaneously and drank.

"Hey Kathleen," the detective said as he slumped back into the armchair.

"Yeah?" *Please don't tell me you want her to join us.*

"You can raise the dead, right?"

Maybe she could, but she certainly wasn't prepared to start a séance now. Not in his condition, not under these circumstances. "No. I can talk to the dead sometimes, but not all the time."

"Can you see if you can contact Jeanette? I'd like to say my goodbyes."

"Sometime, but not right ..."

"Listen," Jacob said.

The room grew silent but for the crackling and popping of the blaze. But then there was another sound, the thumping of helicopter rotors. They had company.

Detective Redmond went to stand, but Jacob reacted quick and steady, the alcoholic glow rapidly exiting his body, replaced by adrenaline. He stood in front of Redmond. "No you don't. Stay here."

"What the fuck," Redmond said. "I'm fucking in charge here."

"Not in this condition," Jacob said as Kathleen quickly grabbed her weapon and approached the door.

Jacob grabbed Redmond's shoulder. "I saved your life last time. Remember? Sit your ass down for a second."

Redmond complied. A fleeting awareness of reality swept over the detective's intoxicated features and he stayed silent.

Kathleen watched the chopper land fifty feet from the front door. "Stay frosty."

But Redmond suddenly had other ideas. He wrenched Jacob's hand away, leaped up, grabbed his weapon, and sprinted out the door.

"NO, NO ... DON'T!" Kathleen shouted after him. But it was too late. Redmond stood outside the chopper, his gun leveled, ready to riddle it with bullets.

The motor slowly thumped to a stop—whop, whop, whop ... whop ... whop—and a loudspeaker suddenly hissed and squealed before a voice boomed out.

"Redmond, put your fucking weapon down! This is your captain speaking!"

Epilogue

Eight months later, Saturday, June 15th, 2:30 pm, Panmure Island beach, Prince Edward Island.

It was a hot, sunny afternoon with a brilliant blue sky and a few thick white clouds floating lazily by. A gentle breeze blew. The steady, rhythmic clapping of the waves on the shoreline was music to Kathleen's ears. Jacob and Reggie Snyden swam in the ocean. Reggie's wife, Lori, lay beside her. They were suntanning on a blanket, leisurely enjoying the day, a cooler of cold drinks within easy reach.

Life is good, Kathleen thought. *Finally.* A lot had happened in the last eight months—hell, in the last two years—and she was thankful for every day she was able to spend on the sunny side of the dirt.

Captain Whiting had come out of the madness a hero, along with Premier Les Simon. Mayor Bob Bolton's death was buried under the carpet as an unsolved murder. Newspaper reports said he was an honest mayor who cared deeply for the health and welfare of his constituents. Reporters went so far as to say he died a hero while handling important details regarding containment and elimination of the Rage Virus.

On that front, things had gone as well as could be expected. At least the entire island had not been destroyed. The zombies had been killed; they numbered almost 30,000 by the time everything was said and done. Miraculously, some of them had even been cured. Like Reggie, whom troops had found unconscious in an alley in Charlottetown and injected with the cure. He had recovered and been cleared of any wrongdoing.

Rex Robertson had been found dead in his laboratory, a bullet from a police-issue nine millimeter Glock imbedded deep in his head. Another unsolved murder.

And the last one, yet to be solved, was the execution-style killing of hitman Bain Derksen, shot three times in the chest in broad daylight while exiting a taxi at the Halifax International Airport.

Kathleen knew Detective Redmond had been a busy man lately. And she also knew, fueled by revenge, he wouldn't stop until it was all over. He had recently departed to the Caribbean to "visit an old friend." She knew, without a doubt, the detective was hunting the last and probably most culpable man on the list, Sid Baillis. She hoped he would hunt him down, kill him, and return alive.

Ovrex Pharmaceuticals was carrying on business as usual. There had been a massive cover-up, starting at the local level and probably going right up to the federal level, for all Kathleen knew. The casino project never got off the ground. She wondered now if the whole thing was a ruse to allow Baillis to infect thousands of locals with the Rage Virus and get rich with the cure.

But she was glad it was over, thankful to be away from the controversy and carnage.

And she was happy to finally be getting settled in her new job teaching autistic children. For the most part, she was tired of psychic readings. They always seemed to result in death and destruction, not to mention the severe emotional toll the job was taking on her. She didn't like the responsibility that went with being able to see into people's futures.

And she had a new boyfriend. Yes, she and Jacob had become an item.

Her last psychic endeavor a few months back had involved Jacob's participation. After they had both recovered from the Rage Virus trauma, their bond became much more intimate. Kathleen finally decided to challenge the only obstacle in front of them. So, one night, she called Jacob over and they performed a séance. She called up the spirits of Mark and Angela, and appealed to their better judgment and good nature.

Kathleen told them they had to continue their journey to the other side and let Kathleen and Jacob move on with their lives. Kathleen would never forget the last image of the two after the thirty-minute conversation. Angela and Mark had joined hands, offered their mutual blessing to the new union of Jacob and Kathleen, and announced they were considering a union of their own in the spirit world. After Jacob and Kathleen offered their blessings, the spirits had faded into the night, arm-in-arm, smiling contentedly.

So they had disposed of their homes, amalgamated their savings, and bought an old Victorian-style home on forty-five acres near Murray Harbour, with their own private beach. Now it was three. And no, three wasn't a crowd. Spike was a welcome addition to the new household.

Kathleen opened her eyes, stretched and looked over at her friend, Lori, looking radiant, toned, and relaxed in her skimpy pink bikini. The two women had become close. During the Rage Virus epidemic, Lori had crawled into an old root cellar of an abandoned house, and lived off canned goods and water until order was restored and she was rescued.

"Hey, girl, I think it's time for a drink," Kathleen said. The cooler sat closest to Lori.

Lori opened her eyes slowly. She had been sleeping. No wonder she looked so relaxed.

"Sounds good," she said sleepily. "What'll it be?"

"Vodka cooler, please," Kathleen said, smiling.

Lori extracted two, closed the cooler, popped the tops with a nearby can opener and handed one to her friend.

"Cheers," Kathleen said, "to our dear friendship. I love you."

"I love you too, sweetie," Lori said, clinking bottles.

They sat up, watching their respective spouses play in the ocean. Jacob came sprinting up to the blanket, dripping wet. "Hey, I'm not going to miss out on that." He reached into the cooler, pulled out a beer, popped the can open and took a long pull.

He darted his eyes back and forth at the women. "Hey, what are you guys all teary-eyed about?"

"Tears of happiness, honey," Kathleen said. "We were toasting our friendship."

"I want to toast that," he said, kneeling down. "To our deep friendship ... and I want to add something: to our relationship, baby. I love you so much."

"I love you too, Jake."

"Cheers," Jacob said. They clinked can and bottles and drank.

Jacob leaned over and kissed Kathleen passionately.

"Whoah," Lori said, grinning. "Get a room."

"Call Reggie if you feel left out," Kathleen kidded.

Reggie was just sloshing out of the water. He stopped, turned to the ocean and took in the infinite and spectacular view out to sea. A flock of seagulls perched on a large rock squawked and simultaneously took flight. As they flew overhead, one precipitously dove down, landing on Reggie's shoulder.

Reggie looked at the bird curiously. "What do you want with me, little guy?"

The seagull stared directly in his eyes for a moment, transfixed. Then it squawked, bit his shoulder, and fluttered away.

"Ouch, you little bastard," Reggie said, noticing a small rivulet of blood dripping from the wound as he approached his friends. "That hurt."

"What's wrong?" Kathleen asked.

"Nothing. Just another beautiful day in paradise. What could possibly go wrong?"

Also by William Blackwell

Phantom Rage, Poison Rage, Infected Rage
Nightmare's Edge
Resurrection Point
Brainstorm
A Head for an Eye
Rule 14
Blood Curse
Black Dawn
Assaulted Souls
Assaulted Souls II
Assaulted Souls III
The Strap
The End is Nigh
Orgon Conclusion
Freaky Franky
The Witch's Tombstone
The Dark Menace
In Your Dreams
Macabre Alley
Tales of Damnation

The End is Nigh Preview

Seven social outcasts flee bloodthirsty gangs and a fiery apocalypse.

"Love this book I've read it like a billion times." -Goodreads

Cray Lenning's life as a garbage collector in a small town is reclusive and boring. Burdened with strong feelings of distrust and resentment, he's content to wallow in lonely self-pity. But when he witnesses a defrocked preacher proclaim "The end is nigh" seconds before getting struck by a car, Cray's world spirals out of control.

Initially, Cray dismisses the wayward preacher as a wacko, but ominous signs begin to convince him otherwise. Enter Sandra Colling, a heartbroken but resolute nurse. Together, they build an underground shelter to try and survive a deadly inferno blazing across the country, and embark on a frantic mission to save others.

Trapped inside the shelter, they learn the terrifying reality of their choices: a traumatized police detective; a manipulative and self-righteous psychologist; a sadomasochistic sex-addict; a rambling, alcoholic preacher; and a mentally ill redneck with an explosive temper.

Their dire predicament worsens when water runs out and they're forced to emerge from the shelter. To survive in this God-forsaken wasteland, they must form an unlikely alliance and battle a far more deadly presence topside—a gang of ruthless escaped convicts, hell-bent on starting an evil polygamist cult that rules by fear, intimidation, and brutal murder.

If you're a fan of Stephen King and Clive Barker, you'll love *The End is Nigh*, a riveting struggle for survival in a savage apocalyptic wasteland.

"Loved it, and highly recommend it." -Amazon

"Underlying the strong plot line is vivid character development and intense examination of relationships and individual motivations." -Goodreads

"This book kept me up all hours, until I had finished it! I could NOT put it down!!" -Goodreads

About the Author

Canadian dark fiction author William Blackwell studied journalism at Mount Royal University and English literature at The University of British Columbia. He worked as a journalist and a newspaper editor for many years before pursuing his passion for storytelling.

His novels have been characterized as graphic, edgy, and at times terrifying. Currently living on a secluded acreage on Prince Edward Island, Blackwell finds much of his inspiration from Mother Nature, odd people, traveling, and bizarre nightmares.

Author Comments

Thank you for reading this book. I would be eternally grateful if you would post a book review on your favorite book retailer website. A positive review is the highest compliment a writer can receive. Reviews are crucial to the success of any author and they also help readers discover new books. You don't have to say much. A few sentences will suffice.

In other news, I have a gift for you. Complete the signup form below with your name and email address and download a FREE copy of *Resurrection Point*, a dark tale about the horrifying consequences of experimenting with death and resurrection.

You're only agreeing to be kept up to date on blog posts, new releases, and freebies. I promise I won't spam you and you can unsubscribe at any time.

Thanks again for your support.

http://www.wblackwell.com/free-ebook/